THE FALLEN

THE FALLEN

THE ELIMINATOR SERIES BOOK 1

MIKE RYAN

WWW.MIKERYANBOOKS.COM

1

DETECTIVE BRETT JACOBS had just gotten back to his office after testifying at the trial of Rich Mallette. Mallette was the leader of a well-known criminal organization that had their hands in just about everything. Drugs, money laundering, extortion, murder, and guns. They had plenty of muscle and liked to use it. They'd been nicknamed Mallette's Maulers for their eagerness in dishing out violence and punishment. Jacobs had worked an undercover assignment for nine months, eventually arresting the big boss on extortion and an attempted murder plot. Mallette was given a fifteen-year prison sentence for his crimes, and he, along with his underlings, had vowed to get revenge on Jacobs for his part in getting the leader convicted.

When Jacobs got back to the office, he was given a lot of high-fives and pats on the back for his work. He didn't do much celebrating, though. It was a big day for him, no doubt, but he tried never to get too high or too low after court appearances. It was a motto that served him well over his past few years as a detective. He was always told to not let a court decision affect him too much, whether it was a victory or a verdict that went against him.

Jacobs started out as a patrol officer as a twenty-one-year-old kid, and after six years in the patrol unit, became a detective. He'd been in the detective unit for the last four years. This past year had been hard on him. Nine of those twelve months had been spent infiltrating the Mallette gang. He was good at his job, devoted to it. Almost to a fault some would say. But he was also devoted to his family. He tried to balance his work and personal life the best he could, though often, it felt like the job usually won out.

Jacobs sat down at his desk and took out a file folder from one of the drawers and placed it on the desk. He opened it up and started moving a few papers around, intently looking for a few more cases to start working on. One of his superiors, Sgt. Buchanan, walked over to his desk and sat down next to him. Buchanan was about ten years older than Jacobs, but they'd become close over the past few years, working together on several cases. Buchanan was almost like an older brother, in addition to being a close friend.

"Getting down to work already?" Buchanan asked.

"A lot more people out there who need to go to the same place Mallette is."

"What're you on? A personal vendetta to get rid of the whole organization?"

Jacobs didn't pick his head up once to look at the sergeant, instead, continuing to focus on the information in front of him. "Maybe I am."

"Are you still worried about that threat Mallette made against you?"

"It's crossed my mind."

"Brett, go home, spend some time with your family. This stuff will all still be here tomorrow. Take a break."

"In jail or not, Mallette's still a very dangerous man," Jacobs said. "Just because he's locked up doesn't mean he's not still able to give orders. You know that. And the people he's still got walking the streets are just as dangerous."

"I know that. All I'm saying is take some time to enjoy that beautiful family of yours."

Buchanan got up and gave Jacobs a pat on the shoulder before he left. Jacobs took his eyes off the paperwork in front of him and thought about what he just heard. He came to the conclusion that the sergeant was right. Nine of the last twelve months were spent away from his family. That was a long time to be away from a wife and three kids, all of whom were under ten. While working the Mallette case, he missed precious family time, moments that he'd never get back. He had a beautiful wife, a nine-year-old girl, and six- and three-year-old boys. And they all missed their father.

3

Jacobs shuffled the papers back into the file folder and returned it to the drawer. He went over to Buchanan's desk and let him know he was taking the rest of the day off, which wasn't technically even necessary considering he was supposed to have the day off anyway. He was only needed for court duty and wasn't supposed to come back to the office. So he went home to be with his family. The Jacobs' lived in a modest condo in Hyde Park, a neighborhood in the south side of Chicago, and located on the shore of Lake Michigan. Hyde Park was one of Chicago's most racially diverse neighborhoods, as well as housing several well-known museums, along with the University of Chicago.

As Jacobs pulled into the designated parking spot in front of their condo, he saw Valerie and the kids sitting on the front steps. He called his wife from the car to let her know he was on his way home. His daughter was a voracious reader and had a book in her hand, like she usually did. His boys were playing with some toy cars and trucks.

"You guys waiting for me?" Jacobs asked as he started walking up the steps.

"I couldn't keep them in," his wife answered.

His kids stopped what they were doing and ran down the steps to hug him. His wife followed them and planted a kiss on his lips. He put his arms around them as they walked back up the steps toward the door.

"Can we go, Dad?" Jenna asked.

"Go? Go where?"

"Please, Dad?" Johnathan said.

Jacobs let out a laugh. "Where are we going? What are you guys asking about?"

"I'm sorry, dear," Valerie said. "I made the mistake of mentioning about possibly seeing a movie today and now that's all they're talking about."

"Oh, well that's OK."

"I know you're probably tired and don't feel like going or anything. I thought maybe I could take them if you wanted to take a nap or something."

"Please, Dad?" Johnathan pleaded again.

Jacobs smiled, not able to say no to the three pairs of innocent eyes looking up at him. "How can I say no to these guys?" he said, rubbing his son's head.

"Yay!" the boys said in unison.

"You're a big softy," Valerie said, giving her husband another kiss.

"Hey, they're good kids. They deserve it."

"You're sure you don't mind?"

"Nah, take them out, have fun. Maybe, um, maybe when you guys get back we can go out to dinner or something. Have some family time together."

"That sounds like a great idea."

"Can we get ice cream too," his youngest, James said.

Jacobs squatted, getting down to his son's level to look him in the eyes. "I think I might be persuaded to include some ice cream in the deal."

"Yay," James said, giving his father a huge squeeze.

"All right, why don't you guys go get ready?"

Feeling good, Jacobs watched as his kids went up the steps. Valerie put her arm through his, locking them together and put her head on his shoulder. Jacobs kissed her on the top of her head.

"How was court?" she asked.

"Good. Let's not talk about it, though."

"Why not?"

Jacobs turned toward his wife and put his arms around her and planted a kiss on her lips. "Because you've given up a lot already. Me not being around, for one. Let's not lose any more of our time together because of the job. Let's just focus on us."

Valerie smiled, liking the sound of that. They kissed for another minute, only the sounds of their children running down the steps breaking it up.

"Sure didn't take them long," Jacobs said.

"They've been looking forward to this all day."

"Maybe if we put them to bed early tonight, you and I can continue this later."

"Sounds good to me," Valerie said, giving her husband one more kiss. "You get some rest. You're gonna need it later."

"I'll hold you to that."

Jenna had already gotten her mother's purse and had it waiting in the car with them as they eagerly awaited their movie outing. As the car pulled out of its spot, Jacobs waved goodbye to his family as they drove away. Once the car was out of sight, Jacobs happily hopped up the steps and into the house. He locked the door, then, like he usually did, put his gun and his badge inside a locked box, then put the box inside a drawer. Then he locked the drawer, too. He'd heard of and known too many stories of kids having an accident playing with a gun and shooting themselves. He was damn sure not going to let that happen in his house.

Jacobs put his phone down on the table and walked into the kitchen and poured himself a cup of soda from a two-liter bottle. He then went back into the living room to put the TV on and plopped himself down on the sofa. He watched an old movie for about ten minutes before lying down, almost instantly drifting off to sleep. It was a brief nap that he desperately needed. Even after being done with his undercover work, he was still working twelve to fifteen-hour days to get ready for the trial, as well as his other work that he needed to get done.

Several hours later, he was woken up by the sound of his phone ringing. Jacobs lay there, his eyes slow to open, just watching the TV for a few seconds. The room looked a little dark to him, and something didn't seem right. He looked to the window, and through a small slit in the curtains, could see that it was no longer light out. It must have been later than he figured. Valerie and the kids should have been back by now, he thought. He looked over at the digital clock on the table. He'd been sleeping for four hours. His heart started beating faster as his mind raced with thoughts that he didn't want to be thinking. Where were they? Why weren't they back yet? He then remembered his phone ringing and thought maybe it was Valerie calling for help. Maybe they had car trouble somewhere.

Jacobs hurried himself over to the window and looked down to their parking spot, hoping to see the car parked there. Maybe they got back and saw he was still sleeping and went for a walk. That's what he hoped for, anyway. He turned back around and rushed over to the table and picked up his phone, seeing that he had several missed phone calls. None from Valerie, though. He had a few calls from other detectives in his unit, including one from Sgt. Buchanan. He also had a few text messages from several of those same detectives, all asking him to call them back. He thought it strange that all the calls and texts were from the last hour. He scrolled to Buchanan's number and called him back first. The sergeant answered almost immediately.

"Brett, where are you?"

"I'm home, why? When I got here, I was beat. Valerie told me to take a nap, and she took the kids to a movie. She actually should've been back by now. I'm starting to get worried about her."

"We've been trying to get a hold of you. You usually pick up right away."

"It looks like everyone in the unit's been trying to get a hold of me. What's going on?" Jacobs answered.

"I'm actually only a few minutes away from you. I'll stop by."

The concern in Jacobs' head had now escalated to a code red alert. He couldn't think of any reason his friend would be stopping by unless something terrible had happened. "Bucky, what's going on?"

"Umm, I don't really wanna say over the phone. I left about twenty minutes ago, so I should be there in about five minutes."

"Left where?"

"I'll, uh, I'll be there in a few minutes, OK?"

Jacobs wanted to keep arguing and make Buchanan tell him what was going on, but something was nagging at him that he already knew. He hung up and immediately scrolled to Valerie's number and called it. As it kept ringing, he prayed that she would pick up. It went to voicemail, though. He hung up and quickly redialed.

"C'mon, pick up, pick up."

It went to voicemail again. Jacobs couldn't shake that voice deep inside that was telling him something was wrong. He tried Valerie's number again, still without any luck. He brought his hand up to his face and started rubbing around his mouth, mostly out of nervousness. A terrified feeling came over him as his heart was pounding, afraid of what Buchanan was going to tell him once he got there. Jacobs went back to the window and looked out at the street as he waited for his friend to arrive. As he waited, he put the phone on speaker and continued trying to reach Valerie, though at this point, it seemed to be a fruitless effort. Nevertheless, he kept trying. Over and over again.

Six minutes went by and Jacobs was getting even more anxious with each passing second. He started fidgeting with his fingers on the curtain, wondering what was taking Buchanan so long to get there. Two more minutes passed until the familiar sight of Buchanan's car parked in front of the building. But that wasn't all. Jacobs was horrified to see a patrol unit car park right behind him. A lump went down his throat as he waited for the three officers to walk up the steps to the house. He couldn't help but feel like they were giving him a death notification. As the officers got near the front door, Jacobs walked over and opened it.

Buchanan stood in the doorway, him and Jacobs staring at each other in the eye, neither saying a word. Nothing had to be said. Jacobs knew what he was there for, and Buchanan, he could already see the pain in his friend's eyes. The tears that were starting to form in Jacobs' eyes did all the talking for him. After a minute of silence, Buchanan thought it would be better if they all went inside.

"Can, uh, we come in?"

"I've been trying to call Val," Jacobs said, hoping beyond hope that the sergeant would say something to alleviate his fears. "I can't get through to her."

"Let's sit on the couch," Buchanan said, putting his arm around his friend.

"Just tell me."

Jacobs took a step back, ready to hear the worst, his eyes glossy. Buchanan took a deep breath as he thought of how to deliver the news. The entire drive there, he tried to think of what he'd say, how he'd say it. But nothing sounded good enough. These types of things were never easy. Even when they notified strangers of unspeakable tragedies, it was difficult. Delivering the same kind of message to a friend was almost impossible. But he knew he needed to say something. He couldn't just stand there in silence and let his friend tear himself to pieces.

"Brett," Buchanan said, trying to keep himself together. He looked at the two uniformed officers, the pain plainly evident on his own face as he continued. "There was, um, something happened."

Buchanan looked toward the floor, unable to get the words out that he needed to. Jacobs took a few more steps back until his shoulder blades knocked into the wall.

"They're dead?" Jacobs asked, tears flowing down both sides of his face.

"I'm so sorry," the sergeant responded, shedding a few tears himself.

"No, no."

Jacobs shook his head a few times, not ready to believe it. He balled both hands into a fist and slammed them into the wall behind him several times as he tried to process the news. Buchanan put his hand on one of Jacobs' shoulders as he tried to console him. Jacobs then slid down the wall until he sat on the floor, pulling his knees up to his face as he buried his head, crying uncontrollably. In his twenty years of experience, Buchanan had seen a lot of people break down in front of him after telling them a loved one had passed away or been killed. But none of them were as heartbreaking to him as this was. He put his hands on his hips, wishing this was nothing but a nightmare, one they'd all wake up from any second. It wasn't a nightmare, though, at least not one that they could wake up from.

Jacobs started rocking in place as he picked his head up, his eyes dancing around the room, not moving in any direction. Then, he suddenly got back to his feet. He wiped the tears from his eyes, an angry look developing on his face. But he lowered his head again, not able to choke back the tears as they streamed down his face again. After a few seconds, he picked his head up.

"Valerie?"

"She's gone," Buchanan softly replied.

Jacobs started moving his head forward and back, letting the back of it hit the wall continuously. "The kids?"

"They're all gone," Buchanan said, barely able to get the words out.

"Oh, God," Jacobs said, putting his hands over his face as he bawled into them.

Buchanan put his hand on his friend's arm. "We'll help you get through this."

"I wanna see them."

"No," Buchanan said, shaking his head. "That's not a good idea."

"I wanna see them."

"You don't wanna see them like that."

"Like what? What happened?"

Buchanan looked down at the floor again and wiped one of his eyes. "They were, um, they were shot."

"Shot?" Jacobs asked in horror.

Up until that point, he had assumed his family was in some kind of car accident. Being gunned down wasn't something that had entered his thought process.

"I wanna see them. Where are they?" Jacobs asked again.

"Not just yet, buddy. Not just yet."

It wasn't an answer that satisfied Jacobs. He suddenly bolted to the front door and tried to run past the patrol officers, splitting them in the middle. The two officers each grabbed hold of him and prevented the detective from getting past them. They held him at bay for a minute, though he tried desperately to get away from them and get out the door, even though he had no idea where his family was at the moment.

"I wanna see them! I wanna see them!"

Buchanan looked at the officers and pointed to the couch, directing them to lead Jacobs over to it. Though he was still trying to get away from them, the two cops led him in that direction, trying to be as gentle as they could with him. They put him on the couch, though Jacobs was still fighting to get away, trying to push the two officers off of him. They were all sitting, but Jacobs was still flailing his legs around as he tried to slip away. Buchanan walked over to him and put his hands on Jacobs' knees to try and calm him down. He opened his mouth, about to tell his friend to relax and take it easy, but he quickly thought better of it. It just didn't seem like the right thing to say at the time. How do you tell someone who just lost everything they held dear in their life to relax or take it easy?

The sergeant tapped Jacobs on the knees, trying to let him know that he understood and was with him. Buchanan couldn't even try to imagine what kind of pain he was going through, but he knew it was immense. All he could do was try to be there for his friend in his most difficult time of need.

2

_____

It took a while for Jacobs to calm down. He was just bursting at the seams, living off of adrenaline at the moment. As the tears started to subside, and reality set in, massive amounts of rage and anger began flowing through his veins. Knowing his family died a violent death, there was nothing he wanted more at that very moment than to find who did it and rip their throats out with his bare hands. He finally stopped struggling with the two officers hanging on him.

"I'm OK," Jacobs said, looking at the two of them.

The two officers weren't so sure, but Jacobs wasn't trying to break free of them anymore. He had accepted that he wasn't going anywhere. The officers had loosened their grip on him, but hadn't let him go completely.

"I'm OK," Jacobs repeated, nodding at them. "I'm OK."

The officers finally released him from their grasp and continued sitting next to him in case he needed to be restrained again. Jacobs took a deep breath and was able to gain control of his emotions. His tears stopped flowing as he wiped the last one from his eye. He looked at Buchanan and sat on the edge of the couch, leaning forward with his elbows on his knees.

"I just saw them a couple hours ago," Jacobs said, shaking his head as he tried to come to grips with what happened.

"I know," Buchanan said.

"I mean, the kids were so happy. They wanted to go to the movies," he said, wiping his eyes as they filled up with tears again.

Jacobs started rocking back and forth as he remembered the last few minutes that he spent with his family. He rolled his hand into a fist and put it into the palm of the other one, holding them against his face as he looked at the floor, remembering the looks on his kids' faces when he told them they could go. After another minute, he was able to get a hold of his emotions again as he took another deep sigh. He kept rocking, trying to release some of his pent-up energy and anger. He looked at Buchanan again, this time wanting answers.

"What happened?"

Buchanan shuffled uncomfortably in his stance as he tried to say it as delicately as possible. "They were shot," he said, throwing his hands up, not wanting to get into all the grisly details.

"Did you see them?"

Buchanan nodded for a second. "Uh, yeah, yeah, I did."

"You still haven't told me what happened."

"I'm trying not to tell you, Brett."

"Why?"

Buchanan shrugged. "Do you really want to know the exact specifics? Think of them, remember them as they lived. Don't let your lasting memories be of what you think they looked like at the end."

"I need to know what happened, Bucky."

"I already told you. They were shot."

"Did they even get to see the movie?"

Buchanan shook his head. "No. No, they didn't."

"Did they even get there? What?" Jacobs asked. His temper was starting to get the better of him. "You gotta tell me something! Would you rather me read about it in the paper or something? Just tell me!"

"They were shot in the car," Buchanan calmly answered.

"In the car? Where?"

"At the movie theater parking lot."

Jacobs looked around the room, like he couldn't quite believe what he was hearing or was having trouble comprehending it. Either way, he wanted more answers.

"So, uh, what happened? Did they see it coming?"

Buchanan shrugged again, clearly not comfortable talking about it or answering his questions. "No, I don't think so."

"How many shots?"

"It's, uh, too soon to say. There were bullet holes all over the place."

His answer drew a stern look from Jacobs, knowing what that meant.

"They didn't even get out of the car?"

"No," Buchanan somberly said. "Looks like the bullets came from the side of the car on the driver's side. The glass was shattered and knocked out on both the front and back windows on that side."

"Have a suspect yet? Recover a gun? Anything?"

"Not yet. Still too soon to tell. It was done with an assault rifle as best as we can figure."

Jacobs let his eyes drift down to the floor, staring at the carpet as he listened intently to the words his friend was saying. It sounded to him like Buchanan wasn't telling him all he knew. It sounded like he was trying to soften the blow, or maybe he was trying to hide something. Or maybe he was just trying to be as delicate as possible, Jacobs thought. His thoughts were swirling in about twenty different directions and he had trouble concentrating on any one particular thought for more than a few seconds. Then his mind turned to who might have been responsible for this heinous crime. And there was only one name that popped up. Mallette.

"We both know who was responsible for this," Jacobs said.

"Mallette was put behind bars, Brett."

"And he and his crew have vowed retaliation against me."

"We're police officers. People vow retaliation against us all the time. They hardly ever follow through with it. Maybe one time in a thousand."

"Mallette's Maulers aren't most people. They have the means and the motive to do something like this."

"I know that's the natural thing to think of, but we don't have any proof of that yet," Buchanan said. "Could it be them? Sure. But let's let things play out first and let the investigation get underway before we start jumping to conclusions."

"This is all my fault."

"Brett, don't go there."

Jacobs shook his head, his face getting more red, looking like he was about to blow. "They warned me. They warned me what would happen. They said if I put their boss away that there would be payback, there would be retribution. And there was."

"Brett, you can't think like that."

Jacobs wasn't really listening to what the sergeant was saying, though. He already had it in his mind that he knew what was going on. "I thought I just had to worry about me. That they'd only come after me. I should've known. I should've known. I should've protected them."

"You can't blame yourself. This isn't on you."

"Yes, it is. It's all on me. It was me who put Mallette away. I knew what they were capable of and I did nothing to stop it. I didn't protect my family. I didn't keep them safe. I put a bullseye on each of their backs."

"I know you're hurting and you're looking for answers, but try not to think of any of that stuff. It's not gonna do you any good," Buchanan said.

"My family was just murdered. My wife, my children, they were innocent. They didn't deserve that fate. Not one bit. And somebody's gonna pay for that. I promise you somebody's gonna pay."

"Brett, don't talk like that. Just try to take it easy."

Jacobs continued sitting there, getting angrier by the minute, bottling it up inside. Buchanan thought it was best to not engage him any further and provoke him more, and just let him try to work off his steam himself. The sergeant then got a call and walked into the kitchen so Jacobs wouldn't hear what was said. It was one of the detectives still on the scene of the Jacobs family murder.

"What's going on?" Buchanan asked.

"Hey, just wanted to let you know we got a break," Detective Garza said.

"What'd you get?"

"I was just inside reviewing the security footage from the cameras on the movie theater."

"Did you see who it was?"

"Oh yeah. We saw the whole thing go down. There was no attempt to cover up or conceal themselves in the slightest. Didn't look like they cared a bit."

"Who was it?"

"Two men. One was Lucky Frazier. Couldn't quite make out the other guy yet. But we'll still go through it and take it back to the office and have it analyzed," Garza said.

"You're sure it was Frazier?"

"Yeah, no doubt about it. After it was over, he walked back to his car and his face was toward the camera. Could easily see it was him. Zoom in on his face and you can even see the scar on the side of his forehead."

"Did his family even see it coming?" Buchanan asked.

"No, thank God. Frazier and his pal came up alongside the car and just started blasting. The kids weren't looking. I think Valerie just started to turn her head as the bullets ripped through the glass."

"Thanks, Rey. Just stay on it."

"Oh, you know it, man. We're not gonna let these crumbs get away with this. You gonna let Brett know what happened?"

"No, not just yet. I don't think he needs to know specifics yet. He's gotta work through his emotions first."

"How's he handling it?" Garza asked.

"Like you'd expect. He's taking it hard."

"I can't even imagine. I'll get Frazier's info out and see if we can run him down, maybe a patrol unit can pick him up somewhere. We'll get to work on identifying the other bum."

"All right. Keep me updated."

"You know it."

Buchanan stayed in the kitchen for a few minutes, thinking about what he'd just been told. Lucky Frazier was a well-known criminal and muscleman for the Mallette crew. His real name was Jay, but everyone called him Lucky after being shot in the head as a nineteen-year-old in an attempted robbery. The bullet glanced off his head, but left a rather noticeable scar. He somehow managed to escape a police shootout, and from that day on, everyone called him Lucky. For escaping both the shootout and the bullet. It was a nickname that Frazier embraced and even insisted on. He soon made a name for himself in the underworld and had no problems delivering blows to his enemies with either his fists or his guns. It was only six months after that police shootout that he joined the Mallette mob. He started out as a regular thug and rose up the ranks over ten years to become Mallette's number one enforcer. And it was a role that Frazier relished and enjoyed.

Buchanan sighed, not sure how he'd explain it to Jacobs should he ask. It was damning evidence that it was indeed retaliation by the Mallette crew. Even though they all suspected that Mallette was responsible anyway, Frazier's picture was positive proof of it. He was Mallette's chief muscle and Frazier didn't do jobs for anyone else. There would be no mistaking who was behind this hit. After standing in the kitchen for a minute, Buchanan finally came back out. Jacobs looked over at him, hopeful that he had more news to report.

"Was that about the case?" Jacobs asked hopefully.

Buchanan hesitated for a second before coming up with a reply. "It was... an unrelated matter."

Jacobs looked disappointed and went back to staring at the floor, his hands on the side of his face. Buchanan felt bad about lying to him, but he believed it was for his own good. He didn't think it would do Jacobs any good just sitting there and stewing about things. It would only make him angrier.

Jacobs looked at the two officers sitting next to him. "You guys can go. I'm all right. I don't need to be babysat. No use in tying up a patrol car here. I'm sure there's other people out there who need help."

The officers looked up at Buchanan, who nodded toward the door, giving them permission to leave. After they left, Buchanan went over to the couch and sat down next to Jacobs.

"You're not alone in this, Brett. We're all with you. Whatever it takes. Whatever you need. All you have to do is ask."

Jacobs glanced at him and nodded, thanking him for the support. Up until now, all he was thinking about was how it affected him. Now, though, he was thinking of the rest of their family. Valerie's parents would be just as devastated. She also had a brother and sister, both of whom had kids of their own. Jacobs had always gotten along pretty well with her side of the family. He wasn't extremely close to them, but they never had any unkind words for each other.

He also thought about his own family. Though his mother had died three years ago, his dad loved Valerie. Mr. Jacobs had adopted her almost like his own daughter. They got along superbly well. Jacobs also had an older brother, Terry, who was married with kids.

"Don't shut me out on this," Jacobs blurted out.

"What?"

"I know you think you're trying to protect me on the details and everything, but I need to know. I need to be kept in the loop."

"Brett, we'll keep you informed. I just don't think it's a good idea if you know every little detail that comes up," Buchanan said. "What good's that gonna do you? All it will do is continue stirring up bad memories and keep you from moving on."

"Moving on? How exactly do I do that? How do I move on from this? How does anyone move on from something like this?"

"It won't be easy. You have to make sure it doesn't consume you."

"Who's taking the lead on this?" Jacobs asked.

"Garza. You know he'll do what he has to do on it."

Jacobs knew Garza was a good detective. He believed he would do a good job bringing the killers of his family to justice.

"You want me to call your dad or brother and have them come down to sit with you?" Buchanan asked.

"No, I'll do it."

"Are you sure? I don't mind making the call for you."

"No. It's my family. It's my responsibility. I'm gonna have to call Val's parents too. And her sister and brother."

"Probably wouldn't be a bad idea if you stayed with your dad or brother tonight. Or the next few days. Probably shouldn't be alone for a while."

"I'll be fine," Jacobs said.

"Maybe. But we all know that when people are by themselves, when they've got too much time to think, that's when the bad thoughts start creeping in. That's when people get hung up. Too much time alone. Don't do that to yourself. Don't think that you're alone in this 'cause you're not."

"I wish it were me. I wish it were me out there. I would give anything to trade places with them. To let them live."

Buchanan put his arm around Jacobs' shoulders. "I know you would."

"When do you have to get back?"

"I can stay a little while. At least until someone in

your family comes. I don't wanna leave you by yourself just yet."

"I guess I should call them now," Jacobs said. "Before they hear it from someone else."

"Just so you know, you don't have to worry about coming in to work for a few days. Policy says you can take three days."

"I'm not even worried about that right now."

"I know. If you need more time, just let me know and I'll see what I can do."

"That's assuming I even come back."

"Brett, don't talk like that. You use this, let it motivate you to come back and bring the criminal element of this city to its knees."

Jacobs agreed, though it wasn't exactly how he was thinking. "There's another way to do that. A more efficient way."

"I'm gonna pretend you didn't even say that. I know you're hurting and a lot of unpleasant things are gonna pass through your mind right now. Just gotta try and work your way through it. Throw yourself into your work for a while. It'll help to ease the pain."

Jacobs wasn't sure if throwing himself into his work would do the trick. He didn't think anything would really ease the pain. Over the past few years he had the unpleasant task of having to inform several people of the deaths of their loved ones. He was always sympathetic for their loss and felt bad for those who had to go on living with the pain of losing those who were close to them. He always thought, though, that he had an idea of the kind of pain that arose from that loss, from having someone ripped away from you suddenly. But now, he knew that he didn't. No one could ever truly know or understand what it was like to have your family torn away at a moment's notice.

Knowing he wasn't doing himself any favors by continuing to sit there and wallow away in pity, Jacobs figured he'd start calling his family members to let them know what had happened. He told Buchanan what he was doing and walked over to the table and grabbed his phone. Jacobs then went into the bedroom and closed the door behind him. He assumed that he'd probably break down again as he told everyone the news and wanted a little privacy when he did.

After watching his friend walk into the bedroom, Buchanan kept staring into the hallway. Being a part of hundreds of murder cases himself, he knew everyone took that kind of news differently. Some swore revenge, some looked numb, and some looked like they were going to have a nervous breakdown. He knew there was no right or normal way to process something like that. But a few things that Jacobs said made the sergeant nervous. Though he assumed it was probably just the shock and suddenness of what happened playing with Jacobs' emotions, Buchanan was a little concerned that his friend might do something he'd regret.

3

IT'D BEEN three days since the deaths of Valerie Jacobs and her children. They had just finished the burial and as everyone began walking away, eventually only Brett Jacobs remained. He stood there, practically frozen, as he looked down at the four graves. Valerie was buried in the middle, with her children on both sides of her. It was still hard for Jacobs to believe that his family was gone. For the past couple of days, he stayed with his father. Though his brother offered him a room at his house, Jacobs just didn't think he could be around too many people right now. With three young kids of their own running through the house, he didn't want to damper everyone's spirits. On the flip side, he didn't want the enthusiasm and energy of a rambunctious family playing games with his depressed mood. He basically just wanted to be by himself and left alone. Valerie's parents, along with her siblings, also offered

Jacobs lodging for a few days, but he declined them too.

Being with his father for a few days enabled him to have some space. His father was never much for talking and usually kept to himself. With Mr. Jacobs being a widower, albeit under different circumstances, he knew to let his son have some time for himself. If he wanted to talk, he'd be there for him. But he knew what his son really needed, and that was time.

As Jacobs stood there, overlooking the graves of his family, he felt he should have said something to them. Something beautiful or elegant, something that would express all the emotions that he was feeling. Something that would be befitting for them. Words that they deserved. But he couldn't think of any of those things. He finally got down on one knee and took turns looking at each of the graves. He started rubbing his face, anxious, trying to think of what to say. Tears filled his eyes.

"I failed you. I failed all of you. You're all here because of the decisions that I made. It should be me in there instead of you. If I could find a way to trade places with you, I would. I would do it in a heartbeat. I... I really don't even wanna go on living without any of you. I miss you all so much already. I don't know what I'm gonna do without you guys. You were my world. You were what got me through each day. Coming home, seeing the looks on your faces."

As the tears streamed down his face, Jacobs rubbed

his eyes and wiped his cheeks with the sleeve of his suit jacket. He was crying so hard that he could barely even see the graves. He continued wiping his eyes until he controlled his tears a little better. They were still falling, but not so hard that he couldn't make out his family in front of him. He then let out a laugh as he started thinking of a few happier times.

"You know, I can still see the looks on your faces when you kids would always beg me to take you out for ice cream. Or Val, when... when you got that weird look on your face when you couldn't remember what you did with your phone," Jacobs said, laughing again. "You always looked so puzzled trying to remember where you put it."

After he stopped speaking, the smile on his face evaporated. The happy look he had slowly diminished. He had no other words to speak at the moment, but he didn't want to leave. Somehow, it felt like he'd be abandoning them if he left. A few dark clouds passed overhead, and few droplets of rain began falling down. Jacobs let the drops bounce off him without giving them a second thought. He didn't even look up. It was a fitting environment, he thought. The burial of his family was accompanied by rain and darkness. That would nicely describe the mood he was in.

Only his father and brother remained nearby as Jacobs talked to his family. Everyone else had gone, even Valerie's family. Valerie's parents tried to stay longer, but they just couldn't stand there anymore and look at their daughter in the ground. Nobody had blamed Jacobs for what happened to his family. Not his own family, not Valerie's, not even friends, neighbors, or coworkers. Nobody blamed him for the deaths of his family. Except for one person. Himself. He doubted that he'd ever shrug off the guilt that he possessed, believing that he was responsible for them being killed. He should have protected them better, he thought.

The rain started coming down a little harder, not that Jacobs paid much attention to it. It really didn't bother him. But his dad and brother walked up behind him with umbrellas in their hands. They stood on opposite sides of him, both putting a hand on his shoulder.

"It's time to go, son."

Jacobs knew he couldn't stay there forever, but he just couldn't bring himself to leave. He just couldn't make his legs move. "I can't."

"Dad's right, Brett. C'mon."

"I can't leave them."

"Listen, I know you're hurting, and that's perfectly normal. But you can't just wither away here. You think Valerie would want that? You know she wouldn't. She'd want you to get on with your life."

Though he stopped crying by that point, the pain was clearly evident on his face and in his eyes. "I don't know how to do that."

"We'll help you. The first step is to get moving. You can always come back tomorrow."

Jacobs' father and brother each grabbed hold of his arms and helped lift him off his knee and on to his feet.

"Why don't you come back to the house?" his brother asked. "Spend some time with us and the kids. It'll do you good."

Jacobs started shaking his head. "No. I just... I can't right now. You know?"

"It's OK. It's OK to be alone sometimes. Just don't spend all your time locked in a room."

Jacobs nodded. With some prodding, he then turned around and started walking to their cars.

"Are you stopping by Valerie's parents for the reception?" Terry asked.

Jacobs shook his head again. "No. I don't wanna see or talk to anybody right now."

"Everyone's gonna wonder where you are."

"Let them wonder. I don't give a damn what anyone else thinks. I just buried my family. I'm sorry if anyone gets upset that I'm not having tea and cake with them."

Mr. Jacobs squeezed his son's shoulder a little tighter. "It's all right, son. You don't need to explain yourself to anyone. Everyone grieves in their own way."

"What are you gonna do right now?" Terry asked.

"Just go back to the house, I guess," Jacobs answered.

"I'll drop you off, son."

They continued walking to their cars. Terry's wife and kids were still in theirs, waiting for him. Terry got in his car as Jacobs got in his dad's car. As his dad pulled away, Terry couldn't help but be worried about his brother. Though he didn't fault him for acting the way he was, he was concerned that Jacobs was going to close himself off from everyone and let the tragedy eat away at him.

There was going to be a reception at Valerie's parents' house for their friends and family, and some members of the police force who wanted to pay their respects. Jacobs just wasn't interested in interacting with anyone. He was appreciative of the people who'd reached out to him so far to let him know that they were with him if he needed anything, but he just didn't want to keep hearing other people speak of Valerie and the kids. Every time he heard their names mentioned, it was like someone was stabbing him in the gut.

Once Mr. Jacobs pulled in front of his son's home, Brett hopped out of the car. He then leaned into the open window to thank his father for the lift.

"You want some company?" Mr. Jacobs asked.

"Nah. I'll be all right. Thanks, Dad."

"Yep. You need something, you let me know."

"I will."

As his father pulled away, Jacobs walked up the concrete steps toward the front door. As he got near the top, he stopped. He let out a sigh as he looked at the house. He hadn't been there in a couple days, since Buchanan told him what happened to his family. He walked up the last remaining steps and unlocked the door and stepped inside. What used to be a warm, lively, and inviting home now seemed cold and lifeless. He kept expecting one of the kids to run into the living room and jump into his arms to greet him. But it wasn't happening. And it would never happen again.

Jacobs walked around the living room and eventually went through every room in the house. He wasn't looking for anything in particular. He just needed to get a feel for the house again. It was almost like he was single again, looking at apartments for the first time. He and Valerie bought the house when she was pregnant for the first time. They pictured themselves living there for the rest of their lives as they raised their children. They envisioned a lot of happy times and memories for themselves. And for a while, they had them. But now, the only memory that was going through Jacobs' mind was seeing Buchanan standing there and telling him his family was dead. He didn't know how he could stay there again. Even for a single night. It just wasn't the same house anymore.

A sick feeling came over him as he meandered through the house. Though he didn't throw up, it sure felt like he had to. He eventually made his way back into the living room and just stood there, his back against the wall. Suddenly, a patch of rage overtook his body, and he couldn't control himself. In one swift motion, he turned and delivered several hard punches with his right hand into the light blue painted drywall. Three small indentations in the wall appeared, where his knuckles had smashed it, and pieces of the wall fell to the floor. He put his bruised and reddened knuckles into the palm of his left hand as he rubbed them. He then rested his forehead against the wall and lightly tapped his head against it several times, almost hoping he was living in a nightmare, and it would somehow wake him up from it.

The rest of Jacobs' day went by much the same way. He had periods of moodiness, highlighted by bouts of rage, punctuated by punching holes in the walls. But outside of the brief periods where he was throwing hands, most of his time was spent sitting on the floor or the couch and staring at the wall, thinking about his family. His phone rang several times, mostly calls from his family or coworkers, trying to make sure he was all right. Jacobs never answered, not wanting to talk to anybody.

As the night rolled on, Jacobs eventually started to watch television, though he really couldn't focus much on it. His mind always went back to his wife and kids, wishing they were on the couch next to him. He tried to eat something, but he just couldn't force himself and wound up settling for a pack of crackers. It'd been an emotional and energy absorbing day for him, and about nine o'clock, Jacobs wound up crashing and fell asleep on the sofa.

Jacobs woke up at seven the following morning and really didn't know what to do with himself. Usually he'd wake up to the sounds of the kids playing around or watching TV, or smelling Valerie cooking breakfast. But there was none of that today. He checked his phone and looked at his text messages and listened to his voicemails. All from friends and other cops who seemed to be concerned about him. He knew he should respond to them and let them know he was OK, but he just tossed the phone back down, not really wanting to talk about it, even in a text message.

Jacobs looked at the time and was still not sure what he was going to do. He knew he was scheduled to be at work, Buchanan made sure to send him several messages reminding him of it. But Jacobs just didn't know whether he was going yet. He knew he should go. He knew that's what everyone wanted him to do, what everyone expected him to do... everyone but himself, anyway. He just didn't know how he could face everyone. It wasn't just everyone looking at him with pity. But Jacobs knew he wasn't the same person. In just three short days, he had been transformed into a dramatically different person. He wasn't even sure if he could still do the job anymore. And he wasn't sure if he wanted to. With all the rage and anger that was flowing through his body, he didn't know if he could think clearly enough, if he could be calm when the situation warranted it, or if he could be impartial.

It wasn't long, though, until he found out. It was just after eight o'clock when he heard a knock on the door. Jacobs wasn't expecting anybody, and nobody had indicated in any of their text or voice messages that they were coming over. He walked over to the window and looked out, seeing a familiar car parked in front of the house. It was Buchanan. He couldn't imagine what he wanted since he didn't say he was coming. Jacobs went to the door and opened it.

"Hey," Jacobs said.

"Well, I guess I've had worse receptions," Buchanan said, noticing the lack of warmth in his friend's greeting.

"What's up?"

Buchanan shook his head. "Nothing. What's up with you?"

Jacobs shrugged. "I'm really not in the mood to play these stupid games right now. What are you doing here?"

Buchanan looked past his friend and noticed a few things that he didn't see the last time he was there. Namely, a couple holes in the wall. "Mind if I come in?"

Jacobs had a displeased look on his face, but still stepped aside and put his arm out to let the sergeant in the door. Buchanan walked around the room a little bit, observing a few of the new round circles in the wall.

"Looks like you added a few things since I last saw the place," Buchanan sarcastically said.

Jacobs didn't feel the need to talk about it. "Mice."

"Really? Hmm. Didn't know they could do this much damage to a place. Chewed right through the drywall I guess, huh?"

"Guess so." Jacobs wasn't in the mood for small talk either and wanted his friend to hurry up and get to the point of why he was there. "So, what are you doing here?"

Buchanan sat down on the couch. "I'm here for you."

Jacobs looked confused. "What? Why would you be here for me?"

"Well, you're going back to work today, right? Figured I'd stop by and pick you up, give you a lift in."

Jacobs didn't seem happy with his friend's reference. "Yeah, I don't know if I'm going in."

Buchanan squinted his eyes like he thought he didn't hear him properly. "You don't what?"

"I don't know if I'm going in," Jacobs repeated.

"Why?"

Jacobs shrugged. "I don't know if I feel like it."

"You don't know if you feel like it? What else are you gonna do? Sit around here all day moping around and feeling sorry for yourself?"

"I've got a right to, don't you think?" Jacobs said, raising his voice.

Buchanan put his hands out, trying to relax and calm Jacobs down. "I know, you do. I'm sorry, that didn't come out right. I'm not trying to belittle or trivialize what happened. But you just can't sit around day after day hoping that all of a sudden you'll feel better. It doesn't work like that."

Jacobs kept shaking his head. "I don't know. I just... I don't know what to do."

"Come back to work. Sitting around here just thinking about everything isn't going to help. You're gonna make yourself go crazy. Immerse yourself in your work for a while until you can clear your mind and get your head right."

"Maybe."

"If you don't, you're just gonna keep thinking bad thoughts and fall into a big, black hole that you can't crawl out of."

Though Jacobs listened to Buchanan speak for a while, he still wasn't sure what the right thing was. Going back to work just didn't seem that important to him anymore. But he also knew that he couldn't sit around the house day after day. While he conversed with Buchanan about his prospects, his positioning altered frequently. He went from pacing, to sitting, to just standing still, then pacing again. Buchanan could see that he was tormented by what he wanted to do. He just hoped that, in a time where Jacobs clearly wasn't himself and was deeply affected by what happened, as he should have been, that he would eventually see that his work still needed him. And he needed it. After another hour of convincing, Jacobs finally agreed to go back to work. Standing against the far wall, he nodded in agreement.

"I guess I'll give it a shot. At least for now."

Buchanan looked relieved. "Good. I'm glad you came to the right decision. You'll see. You're doing the right thing."

"I guess we'll see."

Buchanan waited a little while for Jacobs to get dressed for work. Once he was ready, they drove down to their district to start the workday. Jacobs was unsure what type of reception he was going to get. He wasn't sure whether everyone would feel sorry for him and leave him alone, fearful of bringing up bad memories, or whether everyone would be overly talkative around him in an effort of trying to make him forget the painful events of the past week.

It turned out to be the latter. As soon as he entered the station, it seemed like everyone came up to him to offer their condolences, offer support, or just to tell him how much everyone was with him. It was actually a little smothering; he thought. He probably would have been more comfortable if everyone had just left him alone. After what seemed like hours of greeting everyone he came across, Jacobs finally sat down at his desk, without having to deal with the onslaught of people around him. He stared at his computer screen, not quite knowing what to do at first. He looked around his desk at the couple of files that were placed around the edges. It almost felt like he was on his first day again, unsure of what he should be doing. It wasn't long after that that he was called to the Captain's office. Buchanan came over to him to let him know and escort him there.

Once they entered the office, the captain was already sitting at his desk looking over some papers. Jacobs sat down in the black leather chair in front of the desk, an uncomfortable expression on his face as he wondered what the meeting was about. Buchanan closed the door and sat in the corner of the room. As they waited for the captain to begin, Jacobs turned his head and looked toward his friend for some type of guidance as to what they were there for. Buchanan just nodded and made a face, indicating he had nothing to worry about. After a minute, the captain put down his paperwork and looked at Jacobs for a few moments, sizing up his condition.

"How you holding up?" Captain Whitaker asked.

Jacobs shrugged, not really wanting to talk about his condition at the moment. "Uh, all right, I guess."

"I know it's a tough time for you, but I want you to know we're all with you. Whatever you need, you let someone know."

Jacobs nodded several times quickly, still not in the mood to talk about much.

"You feel good enough to come back right now?" Whitaker said.

Jacobs looked away for a second and shrugged again. Buchanan put his hand over his face, not liking what he was seeing with his friend's body language. "Yeah, I guess, I mean, am I ever gonna feel good enough after this?"

"I don't mean to sound insensitive or anything, but I need to know your head's still gonna be in the game. I understand you're trying to make sense of everything and all that, I get that, I just want to make sure your head's where it should be when you're out there working. You know as well as I do, if you make mistakes, we could lose suspects, get cases tossed out of court, et cetera."

Jacobs looked back at Buchanan again, irritated at the line of questioning. He threw his hands up and was about to get argumentative, but the sergeant recognized the combative posture from his friend and sought to head it off before something was said that would make matters worse.

"Everything's gonna be fine," Buchanan said. "It's just gonna take him a few days to get back into the swing of things."

Jacobs looked back at him and rolled his eyes.

"Maybe if we just keep him on desk duty for two or three days, he'll be ready to go after that," the sergeant said.

Whitaker nodded, though by reading Jacobs' body

language, he wasn't sure the detective was ready to be back in the field. "All right. Give it two or three days. If there's any issues, I wanna hear about it from the both of you."

Jacobs got up and then left the office, Buchanan following closely behind.

"What was the point of that?" Jacobs asked. "It's obvious he doesn't want me back here. What am I doing here?"

Buchanan tried to calm his friend down. "It's not that he doesn't want you back. He just wants to make sure your head's where it's supposed to be."

Jacobs shrugged. "But it's not. I've been telling you that. I don't even know why I'm here."

Buchanan put his arm around him and walked him back to his desk. As Jacobs sat down, the sergeant grabbed a couple of the folders and opened them.

"Here, take some of these, do some legwork, do some research, just get back into the flow of things. Once you start doing things that are familiar, everything will start falling back into place again for you. You just need to start slow, build yourself up again."

"I don't know, man," Jacobs said, still resisting.

"Trust me. Just start working on this stuff, two or three days, you're gonna feel a lot better about yourself."

Another detective walked by and gave Jacobs a pat on his shoulder. "Good to have you back, buddy."

As the detective walked away, Jacobs gave him a

nod. He was back, but it didn't feel right to him. Maybe Buchanan was right, that all he needed was to immerse himself in his work, but it didn't seem that simple. With his wife and kids gone, he felt like there was a big piece of him that was missing, and there was nothing in the world that was going to replace it or fill it back in. He was back, but only in body. He wasn't there in spirit. He was back, but for how long?

4

A MONTH HAD GONE by since Jacobs returned to work. Though he'd gotten back into the normal swing of things, just as Buchanan said he would, he wasn't the same man. And he wasn't the same cop. Everyone could see it. They hoped it was just a phase he was going through, that he'd snap out of it and return to the man and cop he was before, but some of his colleagues weren't sure he'd even be around that much longer to have the opportunity.

Jacobs had always been a pretty mild-mannered person. When dealing with others, he was always polite, respectful, not argumentative. As a cop, he'd always done everything by-the-book. He didn't step on anyone's toes or infringe on a suspect's rights. He did everything the way it was drawn up in the manual. But the past two weeks, he'd been anything but polite and respectful, whether it was dealing with fellow cops, regular citizens on the street, or suspects he was questioning. He seemed to argue with just about everyone and his actions on the job were starting to border on the edge. There'd been several instances lately where he'd been a little more forceful with suspects than he should have been, or than he'd ever been before. Most of the other detectives and police officers brushed it off, thinking that he never quite crossed the line.

But Buchanan wasn't one of those. He was getting deeply concerned about the mental state of Jacobs. He thought by Jacobs investing himself into his work, that his mood would eventually pick up. Buchanan knew it would take his friend some time. Anyone in the same situation would go through the same battles. But he wasn't counting on Jacobs showing more aggression. That was the most alarming thing that Buchanan was concerned with.

A group of detectives, including Jacobs and Buchanan, had just gotten back to the office after raiding a house and questioning a few suspects who lived there. They acted based on a tip by an informant that they weren't sure was accurate, but rolled on it nonetheless. Unfortunately, nothing came out of it. Nothing except another display of Jacobs' ever-growing reliance on the use of force. Almost immediately after sitting down at his desk, Buchanan came over to him.

"You wanna tell me what that was all about?"

"What?" Jacobs asked, though he knew what he was referring to.

"You grabbed a guy by the shirt collar and tossed him up against the wall. I thought you were gonna slug him into next week."

Jacobs shrugged it off. "I wasn't gonna hit him."

"Sure could've fooled me."

"I just wanted to put a little scare into him."

"Well, it sure worked. On the both of us."

"Well, I didn't, so I'm not sure what the problem is," Jacobs said.

"The problem is that these little incidents have been happening pretty frequently lately. You're toeing the line on what's acceptable, Brett."

"Then write me up."

"One of these times, you're gonna lose your cool, and you're gonna wind up in the principal's office. And I'm not gonna be able to get you out of it."

"I'm not asking you to."

Buchanan sighed, not liking his friend's answers. He had a feeling something else was at play. "So, what's the reasoning behind all the heavy-handed stuff?"

"Why's there gotta be a reason?"

"Because you were never like that before," Buchanan answered. "There are some guys who get away with stuff like that. The hotheads. That's never been you. Never been your style."

"Well, maybe it's about time I started making it my style. Gets results."

"Does it?"

"You do things your way, I'll do it mine," Jacobs said.

"What else is eating at you? It's gotta be something. You didn't just all of a sudden decide to change your tactics. What's tugging at you?"

Jacobs looked at the files on his desk, unsure whether he really wanted to get into it at the moment. But after a minute, with his new combative demeanor, he figured, why not?

"Fine. You really wanna know what's pissing me off?"

"That's why I asked," Buchanan said.

"It's been over a month since Val and the kids were killed. We haven't made one step towards an arrest, a conviction, nothing! Not one stitch of progress has been made. Not one. We're not any closer to nailing someone than we were a month ago."

"These things take time, man, you know that."

"Bull! We don't need time. We know who did it, we know who set it up. Mallette ordered it, Frazier carried it out. Doesn't take a rocket scientist to know that," Jacobs said, a little hot under the collar. "We got Frazier on video for crying out loud."

"As far as Mallette is concerned, knowing it and proving it are two different things. We need evidence. We don't have it yet. But we will. And you know it takes time to get it."

Jacobs started squirming around in his seat,

looking increasingly agitated by the second. "Yeah. Proof. Evidence. Don't rough anyone up. Play by the rules. The guilty are always protected."

"Brett, you know that's not true."

"Sure it is. And what about Frazier?"

"What about him?" Buchanan asked.

Jacobs threw his arms up. "We know it was him. We saw him plain as day."

"He's gone underground somewhere. We've got alerts out on him if he tries to take a plane or a bus or something. He just hasn't turned up yet. But he will."

Jacobs shook his head, not liking anything that he was hearing. Buchanan knew it was a frustrating time for him. All he could advocate doing was to keep plugging away, hoping that something would break their way soon.

"I know you're looking for closure," Buchanan said. "I know you want everything wrapped up yesterday and I don't blame you for that. But we all know it's very rare that things move along this quickly. We'll stay on it, we'll keep pounding the pavement, we'll keep talking, we'll keep interviewing, we'll keep questioning, we'll keep doing all of those things. Eventually, we'll get the break we need. Something or somebody will break. And then we'll pounce. And then... you'll get the justice that you want."

It all made sense to Jacobs, and he knew it was the right thing for the sergeant to say, but he wasn't sure he believed any of it. At least not in this instance. "I'm not even sure if justice is what I want."

Buchanan looked a bit thrown off by the suggestion. "Then what else would you be looking for?"

"Revenge."

Looking as alarmed as ever at what he was hearing, Buchanan leaned forward and balled his fists together, putting his knuckles on the desk for support. "Listen, I don't wanna ever hear you talking about revenge again. I don't know whether you actually mean or believe that or not. But these are crazy times we live in. Someone catches a police officer talking about getting revenge on tape or a microphone and they'll throw the book at you."

Jacobs didn't respond verbally and just did a quick nod.

"Now I don't know if you truly believe that or if it's just the sorrow in your heart," Buchanan said. "Either way, get it out of your system and don't let it back in."

Once again, Jacobs didn't respond, except for a nod to let the sergeant know he heard him loud and clear. But that didn't mean he liked or agreed with him. Or that he was about to do as was suggested to him. Hoping he'd gotten through to him, Buchanan then left to attend to other issues, leaving Jacobs alone with his thoughts. Jacobs leaned back in his chair and just watched some of the other detectives move about the office, thinking about some of his options. If only Buchanan could have known what was ruminating inside of Jacobs' head at that very moment, he probably would've wound up lighting into him with a verbal assault for another twenty minutes.

Jacobs stared at his computer screen for the next few minutes, thinking about his future. As far as he was concerned, he didn't think he had one. He certainly didn't have any on the home front, not without his family. And he wasn't interested in ever having another one. He couldn't imagine falling in love with someone else. Not in a year, not in five years, not in twenty years. There was only one woman for him. And now she was gone. And the rest of his life went with her. He could do as Buchanan suggested, and just pour himself into his work, but that didn't seem to be that appealing either. Maybe for a few months or so that could work. But not for a long-term future.

He had to give some thought about what would truly make him happy again. Or, if happiness was something that he would never feel again, at least what would make him content? And though Jacobs knew it wasn't right, he knew it wasn't what anybody wanted to hear, and he knew it wasn't what he should've been feeling, he kept coming back to one thing. Revenge. That's what he truly wanted. He didn't want to see anyone arrested or behind bars. He wanted to see them dead. And he wanted to be the one who pulled the trigger. Mallette, Frazier, his partner, and anyone else who had a hand in what happened to his family. At that moment, Jacobs didn't care about justice. He wanted revenge. And he wanted it badly. The longer he thought of it, the more he could envision himself with Mallette or Frazier standing in front of him, and him being the one to pull the trigger on them. That's what would get him through.

As he contemplated the future, and whether he wanted to start taking the law into his own hands, he thought about what his actions would mean. He could kiss his job goodbye, for one. And seeing or talking to the rest of his family was something that wouldn't happen very often, if it all. He also had to think about his own mortality. Whether that was something he was prepared for. He knew that if he went down the road he was thinking of, there was a good chance he'd wind up dead at some point. With the amount of damage he was intent on inflicting, he'd wind up getting caught up in some chaotic and hair-raising situations that he might not walk away from.

It only took Jacobs a few minutes to decide that he was ready and prepared for whatever might result from his actions going forward. He wasn't really that concerned with his own life at that point. The only thing that really concerned him was making sure that the people responsible for taking his family's lives paid the price for it. And he was determined that they would. If it wouldn't be at the hands of the law, it would be from his own. But if he was going to embark on his own endeavor, Jacobs knew he'd need some extra equipment. Guns, ammunition, bulletproof armor, and accessories. And he had a good idea where he could get some of it: Eddie Franks. Franks ran a pawn shop, but often conducted illegal business out of it. He was on the police radar, but they never were able to get enough evidence to make any charges against him stick.

Jacobs went on the computer and visited a few websites where he knew he could purchase some armor. He bought a Farm Coat, which was constructed with removable ballistic panels placed in the front and back of the jacket to protect vital organs. With two inside pockets, two chest pockets, and two hand pockets, it was enough to hold a fair amount of gear. Jacobs thought it was perfect for him. It weighed about eight pounds, had removable Kevlar interior lining, and was able to stop various types of bullets, including a .45, 9mm, hollow-points, as well as .44 and .357 Magnums. At just a shade under a thousand dollars, Jacobs bought it immediately to have shipped to his house. He then looked at more traditional bulletproof vests, though he was looking for something with a little more protection than the standard police-issued ones. He noticed one that also had a flap to cover the groin area, as well as the throat, and also had sleeves on it to cover the biceps area. It was a nice touch to have the added protection in those areas that the normal vests didn't cover. Even though it cost eleven hundred dollars, it was a must have as far as Jacobs was concerned.

Jacobs had about thirty-thousand dollars in his

bank account, but he knew that wouldn't last long if he kept making expensive purchases. Guns, ammunition, and other accessories, he would have to pick up somewhere along the way. If he sold his house, he'd be able to sock a little more money away, but someone else would have to do it for him. He'd probably be a wanted man by that point. And that brought up a new set of issues for him. He'd have to find someplace else to live. That part didn't really bother him too much. He'd been thinking about that for weeks, anyway. Going home to an empty house every day was growing less appealing all the time. Especially one that had been so full of life for a long time.

The longer Jacobs sat there, the more convinced he was at what he wanted to do, what he wanted to accomplish. He wanted to fight fire with fire. You couldn't fight the likes of Mallette's Maulers by trying to be on the right side of the law. He and his family were proof of that. It just didn't work. They didn't fear the law and didn't think they could be caught. The only thing that group would understand is pain. And he would bring it.

Jacobs knew that he had to act now. The longer he waited, the more chances it gave him to talk himself out of it. And it was something he didn't want to talk himself out of. This is what he wanted. He was through with the law and what it represented. And he was OK with wherever that decision took him. Not wanting to waste any more time, Jacobs wrote down Franks' address and started to rush out of the station. Buchanan had just picked up a folder from another detective for a case they were working on and happened to be going in Jacobs' direction, though Jacobs didn't see his face. All he saw was a body walking toward him. Buchanan could see that his friend seemed preoccupied with something and grabbed his arm as they passed each other.

"Hey, where you going?" Buchanan asked.

"Oh, just got a lead on something. Wanna go check it out."

"Oh. Great. What kind of lead?"

"Uh, well, I don't wanna say too much about it yet until I see whether it pans out or not," Jacobs said. "No use getting worked up about anything until I know for sure."

Buchanan thought he sounded a little vague, more so than normal. But he figured it could've still been his emotions playing with him. "OK. Well, let me know if you get anything from it."

"Yeah. Sure will."

After leaving the police station, Jacobs got in his car and started driving. But instead of heading for Franks, he missed the turn, and went in a different direction. It was almost like he was being pulled in that other direction. He eventually wound up turning into the cemetery. It felt like Valerie was calling to him, asking him to come. Once Jacobs parked, he sat in his car for a few minutes, staring at the graves that lined the grassy area.

Jacobs finally got out and walked around the graves until he got to the one that was special to him. Once there, he got down on his knees. For some reason, he seemed nervous, afraid to say what he wanted to say, like she was actually there in front of him, able to respond. Jacobs reached down and grabbed a handful of grass, rubbing it with his fingers and letting it fall back down to the ground. He looked at the headstone and finally was able to find his voice, though he still struggled to find the right words.

"I, uh, I'm not really sure what I'm doing here."

Jacobs started rubbing his hands together as he searched for the proper words. He then looked up at the sky, hoping some inspiration would hit him. He felt a tear in the corner of his eye and wiped it away.

"I guess I'm just here 'cause... I guess I'm feeling guilty. Guilty about what I think needs to be done," Jacobs said, dabbing his eye again. "I'm about to do some things, Val. Things I know you wouldn't like. Things I know you wouldn't approve of."

He stopped for a minute, shaking his head, continuing to wipe his eyes. He took a deep sigh before opening up again.

"I hope you're not looking down on me right now and feeling different about me. I just... I just don't know what else to do. I miss you. I miss the kids. And I don't know how to move on. I don't know how to get rid of the pain. It hurts not having you guys around anymore. I guess maybe I'm just looking for a way to get that feeling of emptiness out of me."

Jacobs was able to compose himself a little better and looked around to see if there was anybody else nearby. There wasn't. There were a few people visiting graves off in the distance, but nobody that was close to him. He turned his attention back to Valerie.

"I'm gonna make people pay for what they've done. I know that's probably not the way I should handle it, but I don't know how to live without you. Maybe I just came here 'cause I wanted your blessing. I don't want you to think I've become some kind of monster or something. I don't know when I'll be able to get back here next. It might be awhile."

Jacobs smiled as he thought of his wife.

"Who knows? Maybe I'll be lying there next to you soon."

5

JACOBS ARRIVED at Eddie's Pawn Shop and walked into the small establishment. He looked around a little bit as the man behind the counter helped the only other customer in the store. Jacobs followed the customer as he left the store, closing the door after he exited. He locked it and flipped the open sign that hung on the door so it read closed to anybody passing by. The man behind the counter had been watching the man closely and was stunned at him closing the store.

"Hey! Hey, what are you doing?"

Jacobs saw there was a shade at the top of the door and pulled it down. The man behind the counter was starting to get worried about what was happening, thinking he was about to get robbed.

"I have a gun behind the counter, man."

Jacobs pulled his jacket back, revealing his own gun. "So do I."

"I don't have much money here. It's been a slow day."

"Relax, I'm not here for your money," Jacobs said, slowly walking toward the counter.

"Then what do you want?"

"I take it you're Eddie Franks?"

"Depends on who's asking."

Jacobs took out his badge and showed it to him. "I am."

"I guess it wouldn't do any good to say that he just left for the day?"

Jacobs pulled out a piece of paper and put it on the counter. It was Franks' picture. "No, I don't think so."

Franks sighed, figuring he was being ramrodded for something. "Aww man, what do you want? I haven't done nothin'."

"Oh yeah?" Jacobs said, walking around the counter. "Didn't you say something about having a gun back here? With your record, pretty sure that's illegal."

"C'mon, man, you're not really gonna run me in for that, are you?" Franks asked, leaning back against the wall to give the cop some space.

"Well, it is against the law," Jacobs said, finding the gun and picking it up.

"I mean, you know how it is. Working in a place like this, you never know who's gonna walk through them doors. A man's gotta protect himself."

"Well, maybe we can come to some kind of arrangement."

"What kind of arrangement?"

"I'll forget about the gun if you tell me what I want to know."

"Which is?" Franks asked.

"I need someone who's good at creating and forging false documents."

"I don't know anything about that stuff, man. You're asking the wrong guy."

"I'm asking the right guy," Jacobs replied. "You've got a history of that type of deal."

"Nah, man, c'mon, that was like a lifetime ago. Yeah, I did some business like that a long time ago, but not no more, man. I mean, after I got out of the joint, I left that life behind. That's why I started up this place."

Jacobs looked at him stone-faced, not believing a word of it. "You really expect me to buy that crap you're spewing?"

"It's the truth, man."

"The only truthful part of that is you spent time in jail."

"C'mon, man, give me some credit. You think I'm gonna risk going back there over whatever it is you think I'm doing? I swear to you I'm on the straight and narrow."

Jacobs couldn't help but let out a laugh. "Do I look like this is my first day on the job?"

"I dunno, man, what do you want from me?"

"Listen, I'll be straight with you. I don't give a damn about anything you're doing outside of here. As a matter of fact, I hope you are because I think you can help me."

"Hey, even if I was doing what you think I am, I wouldn't give up any of my contacts to you," Franks said. "It'd eventually get back to me that I sold them out and I could count on one hand the number of days I got left living after that."

Jacobs walked back around the counter, thinking of his next play to get Franks to give up his contacts. He knew it wouldn't be easy convincing him that he wasn't with the police anymore and that he meant him no harm. He thought of what he could say or do to make him change his mind. As he tried to think of different options, one thing kept plugging away at him. Maybe he should just tell him the truth. No games or tricks, just the plain honest truth. He saw a stool at the end of the counter and hopped onto it.

"Sit down," Jacobs said, motioning for him to grab another chair.

Franks hesitated, not sure what the cop was up to. Seemed like different interrogation tactics than he was used to. But, he eventually complied and sat down on a stool on the opposite side of the counter. Both men leaned forward on the counter, putting their arms and elbows on them.

"So, here's the deal," Jacobs said, finding it tough to put into words and actually admit what his plans were. He took out his badge again and tossed it around in his hand for a minute, mulling over what he was about to do with it. "See this?" he asked, holding it up for Franks to see.

Jacobs then saw a garbage can against the wall. He flicked his wrist and sent the badge flying into the air, crashing into the wall and dropping into the wastebasket. Franks wasn't sure what was happening.

"What'd you do that for?"

"'Cause that's where it belongs," Jacobs said. "In the garbage. I'm through with the law. I'm not a cop anymore. I walked out on that about an hour ago."

"Hmm. Do they know that?"

"They will soon. That's why I need you. I'm planning on doing some things and I don't plan on getting caught."

Franks looked at him curiously, still not sure everything was on the level. "You sure I'm not being set up for something?"

"Well, even if you were, I'm pretty sure you could argue this is entrapment, so I doubt anything would stick on you anyway."

"Oh."

"So, what do you say?" Jacobs asked. "Are you willing to help me?"

Franks scratched his face as he thought about it. He still had some alarm bells going off. "I don't know. Assuming I could help... and I'm just assuming that I could, exactly what is it that you're looking for?"

Jacobs took a deep sigh as he thought about it. "Well, probably need some false identification, that way my name doesn't show up in any system if I need to show ID for something. Could probably use some extra guns and ammo. All I got is what's on me."

"That all?"

"Yeah, for now. Oh, and uh, I'd prefer them to be cheap or free. I'm running low on funds. Just spent a couple thousand on bulletproof vests and coats."

Franks raised his eyebrows at the request. "Well, unless you can go down to the neighborhood Goodwill store, I'm pretty sure you're not getting any of that for cheap or free. I mean, not unless you're planning on killing someone and taking what they got."

Jacobs glared at him, not totally against the idea. Franks said it as a joke and laughed, but quickly stopped when he saw the police officer looking at him.

"I wasn't really serious with that, you know," Franks said.

"So, can you help me?"

"Maybe. Just what exactly do you plan on doing? Killing someone and skipping out of town or something? Laying low for a while?"

Jacobs shook his head. "I plan on killing a bunch of people. Laying low isn't exactly what I had in mind."

Franks' eyes widened upon hearing he was intent on killing a lot of people. Even though he was a shady character, he still had his limits. "You're not planning on taking out the rest of the cops at your station or anything, are you? I mean, I don't have a love for cops or anything, but that would just seem crazy. Or the local school or anything?"

"You know Mallette's Maulers?" Jacobs asked.

"Yeah, I know them. Who doesn't?"

"Well, I'm gonna kill every single one of them."

Franks squirmed in his seat. "Now that's just plain old crazy talk. You know how dangerous that clan is? Of course you do, you're a cop."

"Ex-cop."

"Whatever. You're planning on going up against that crew?" Franks said, looking around the store for emphasis. "I don't see anybody else here with you. And I know you can't be crazy enough to take on that group all by yourself."

"Why not?"

"Why not? Why not? 'Cause they're a bunch of nut-jobs, that's why not," Franks said. "They'll kill you, cop or not, long before you ever reach their front door. They're a nasty, evil, bunch of people, man."

"So, I take it you don't do business with them?" Jacobs asked.

"Nah, man, I don't mess with them people. I mean, I've worked with them once or twice in the past, and I mean way in the past. Like years and years ago. I stay as far away from that bunch as I can. And I'd advise you to do the same."

"Well, thanks for the advice, but I don't plan on listening to it. I'm still gonna take them out."

Franks looked dumbfounded at the suggestion and

shook his head. "Man, that's a tall order for anyone. If that's what you're hell-bent on doing then I wish you luck, brother. If you want, I'll say a word or two at your funeral. That is, if there's anything left of you to bury after Mallette's Maulers are done chopping you up."

"Your concern for my safety is heartwarming, but that doesn't change what I gotta do. If you're afraid of that bunch, that's fine, but that's not gonna stop me."

"Why are you so intent on going against them, anyway? Lose a case against them or something?"

Jacobs shook his head. "No, there's a little more to it than that. They're responsible for murdering my wife and children."

"Oh, wow," Franks said, looking genuinely saddened by the news. "Wait, are you that cop that I heard about in the news? Happened like a month or so ago?"

Jacobs sighed. "Yeah. That was me."

"Aww, man, I'm sorry to hear that. What a rotten thing to go through."

"Yeah. So that's my story. That's why I wanna hit Mallette's Maulers."

"I feel for you, brother, I really do, but man, I think you got yourself some kind of death wish there."

"Well, whether I do or not, that's my call," Jacobs said.

"I hear ya on that. Wait a minute, wasn't Rich Mallette sent to prison a little while back?"

"Yeah, but he still ordered it."

"Oh, no doubt there, no question about it. I'm just saying, if you're jonesing on going after his crew, you're gonna have to wait awhile to hit the big boss. Unless you're planning on taking him out in prison."

"I can wait on him. I actually prefer him to be last," Jacobs said. "I want him to know I'm coming. I want him to see the rest of his crew fall, one by one. I want him to worry."

"Man, you really wanna go full on crazy with this, don't you?"

"They killed an innocent woman. Three innocent children. I'm not gonna let them get away with that."

"Dude, I totally feel you on that. The pricks should get what's coming to them for that. I just gotta say though, you're a cop, and that's not exactly a cop-like thing to do."

"I told you, I'm not a cop anymore. I just quit."

"But why?" Franks asked. "You're throwing away your career. Why not just let the law take its course?"

"Because the law doesn't always work. You should know that."

Franks titled his head, understanding his point. "Yeah, you're right about that. But still?"

"And because I don't wanna see them behind bars. I wanna see them underground."

"I feel your pain, man, I really do."

"So, about that help?" Jacobs asked.

Franks was almost convinced that Jacobs was on the level by that point. But still, there was always a little something in the back of his mind telling him to be wary. That's probably why he was still in business and evaded police for as long as he had.

"You're totally sure this is on the level?" Franks asked.

"I'm totally sure."

"'Cause I got cameras in here, rolling, picking up this entire thing. Just between you and me, I got a recorder too that picks up on the conversation. Helps in business activities, if you know what I mean."

"It's not a trick."

"All right, I'm just making sure. 'Cause I can play back this entire thing if I have to. Or I can erase the whole damn thing so you got nothing on me."

"I'm not interested in hurting you," Jacobs insisted. "Just want what I asked you about."

Franks scratched his face again, analyzing the man sitting before him. The alarm bells had been silenced, and he believed everything he was being told. He didn't think the cop was just trying to pull one over on him.

"OK, here's what I'll do," Franks said, getting off his stool and reaching under the counter. He took out a piece of paper and pen and slid it over to Jacobs. "Write down your name and number and I'll pass it along to see if someone can help you out."

Jacobs grabbed the pen, but was hoping for something more immediate. "I have to wait?"

"That's how it works, my friend."

"I was hoping to get something done today."

"Well, maybe it'll be today, maybe not. They'll do some checking on you to make sure your story checks out."

"What, you think I'm lying?" Jacobs asked.

"Nothing personal, man, we just gotta take precautions. There's a reason we're considered the cream of the top."

"I think you mean crop."

"Whatever. It's because we don't just fall over and bow down to whoever walks through that door. Can't be on top when you're in the slammer, know what I mean?"

Jacobs nodded. "I understand."

"You on a time frame?"

"Well, considering I just walked out on my job, the sooner the better."

"I'll see if they can put a rush on it," Franks said.

"Thanks."

"In the meantime, if you want some guns, there's a place up the street. Dry-cleaning store. Called Harry's."

"A dry-cleaning store called Harry's?" Jacobs asked. "And they sell guns?"

"Well, sometimes." Franks leaned forward across the counter and started looking around and whispering, as if he was afraid that someone else was listening. "Just between you and me, it's just a front."

"It is?"

Franks scrunched up his face and closed his eyes

and nodded. His face indicated he was almost proud to let the cat out of the bag. "They're dry-cleaning prices are extremely high."

"So?"

"So, it scares the legitimate customers away. If you stake out the place for a week, you'll notice they never have anybody walking through the doors. At least, nobody with clothes. You might see some bags that have some weapons in them, though."

Jacobs nodded several times. "Thanks for the tip."

"You didn't hear that from me."

"Why? Not in business with them?"

"Nah, bunch of creeps," Franks answered. "Bunch of guys who walk around and think they're bigger, tougher, and badder than they really are. Nothing but a bunch of punks, really."

"Maybe I'll pay them a visit, then."

"Well, if you do, make sure you got your hand on your gun."

"Why's that?"

"They don't particularly care for people they don't know walking in there unless they already set it up beforehand. So if you go, tread carefully."

"I'm done treading carefully," Jacobs said.

"Suit yourself. Just figured I'd give you the warning."

"Thanks."

Jacobs finally filled out the paper by writing down

his name and phone number on it. Franks picked it up and studied it for a few seconds.

"If you're gonna go through with this, you're probably gonna wanna ditch that phone."

"Oh. Yeah, I didn't even think about that," Jacobs said.

"No worries. I got some here you can buy. If everything goes through, I can give you one the next time you're here."

"Works for me."

"That's about it. I'll give you a call if something gets set up," Franks said.

Jacobs got up off his stool and walked over to the door to unlock it. Once he left, Franks hurried over to it, putting the shade up, and turning over the sign to read that the store was open again. He looked out the door and saw Jacobs walking up the street toward the dry-cleaning store.

"You're one crazy son of a bitch," Franks said to himself. Then he smiled. "I like it."

Franks went back to the counter and grabbed his phone to call one of his contacts.

"Sang, might have a new job for you," Franks said. "Name is Brett Jacobs."

6

JACOBS REACHED Harry's Dry Cleaning and stood a few stores down from the business, just staking it out for a while. Just as Franks had told him, Jacobs didn't see one customer enter or exit the store. He stood there for close to an hour, even walking past the entrance a few times, taking a glance through the window to get a sense of what lay inside. After the hour was up, Jacobs didn't feel like wasting any more time. Part of the reason he waited so long was to try and get a sense of how many people were inside. He'd hate to get into trouble if there were twenty people inside. But, there was no way of telling. Not unless he waited all night, and there was the possibility that they stayed all night, or even ducked out the back door. He figured he'd just have to go inside and wing it.

Jacobs stood at the door and took a deep breath. He

then felt the handle of his gun and took it in and out of its holster a few times, making sure it didn't stick if he needed to use it quickly. He swung the door open and confidently walked inside. There was a man sitting at the counter, drinking a soda and reading a magazine. He didn't look too concerned about greeting anyone walking through the door. Once he looked up and saw the strange man, he was a little alarmed. Usually anyone who came in was known to them.

"We're not accepting new customers," the man said. "We're all booked up for the next few weeks. There's another place the next block over."

"Yeah, but I don't think they have the service that I'm looking for."

The man looked at Jacobs, thinking he looked like trouble. He noticed he didn't have any garment bags with him.

"And what kind of service is that?"

"Steel and lead," Jacobs answered.

"That's a new one, man, don't know anything about that. Try that other place."

Jacobs walked closer to the counter. "Nah, I think I'll try this one."

The man behind the counter stood up, ready for a fight, and actually kind of hoped he'd be able to dish out some punishment. Jacobs seemed a little too cocky for his tastes.

"Listen, man, I'm trying to do you a favor. Turn

around and walk out that door before something bad happens to you."

"Oh, a concerned citizen," Jacobs said. "Nice of you to look after your fellow man like that. But I think I'll stay."

The other man was getting ticked off and walked around the counter, ready to start firing some punches in Jacobs' direction. Before things escalated too much, Jacobs reached into his jacket to get his badge. Then he remembered he just tossed it in the trash at the pawn shop.

"Oh crap," he thought to himself. "Why'd I do that?"

If Jacobs had been thinking more clearly, he would have taken the badge out of the trash before he left so he could use it to his advantage. Obviously, he wasn't thinking things clearly and was just flying by the seat of his pants without a clear plan. Now, he had to come up with something else. Then he thought of his ID card. Should still do the trick, he thought. He reached into his pocket and removed his police card and held it out for the man to see.

"Police," Jacobs said.

The man took a few more steps toward him and stared at the card. A displeased look overtook his face, a little unhappy that his chance to inflict some pain on the man was seemingly over.

"So, what do you want?"

"I hear you guys are dealing guns out of here," Jacobs said.

The man laughed, trying to play it off. "Guns? Man, look around, you see any guns here? We're a dry-cleaning store."

Jacobs looked around and noticed a closed wooden door behind the counter.

"What's back there?" Jacobs said, pointing to the door.

"Back there? Just clothes and stuff."

Jacobs started moving forward. "Mind if I take a look?"

The man put his hands on Jacobs' chest to prevent him from going any further. "Yes, I do mind. You got a warrant?"

Jacobs shook his head. "No, not right now."

"Then you ain't looking back there right now."

"Maybe I wanna do a little business."

"Sorry. We don't serve police here."

"Well, that's not very friendly like. How many people you got back there?"

"I don't think that's your business."

"So, is this your operation or are you just the stooge?" Jacobs asked, hoping to get a rise out of him.

The man didn't appear amused and by the look on his face, seemed like he just wanted to start punching Jacobs in the face right there.

"Never mind, that was a silly question," Jacobs said. "Of course you're not anyone important. If you were, they wouldn't have you sitting out here, drinking soda and reading women's magazines."

That was enough to push the man over the edge. Cop or not, he wasn't taking that kind of insult from anyone. He reached back and tried to connect with a right hand on Jacobs' face, but the former police officer blocked it with his left forearm. Jacobs then drilled the man flush in the nose with a right hand of his own. With the man stunned and holding his nose, Jacobs then unleashed another punch, nailing the man across his cheek and eye. The man stumbled back into the counter, clearly hurting. Not knowing how many other people were in the building, if anybody, Jacobs didn't want the fight to go on too long. They were bound to raise a considerable amount of noise from the dust-up, which would bring more of the man's friends into the fray. Jacobs wasn't interested in getting into an all-out brawl at the moment.

Jacobs wanted to end the incident now and took a firm hold of the back of the man's head. He then drove it into the counter, quickly knocking the man off his feet from the force of the blow. Jacobs tapped the man in the stomach with his foot to see if he was still with it, but the man wasn't moving. Jacobs could see that he was still breathing and apparently had just been knocked out. With the man no longer a threat, Jacobs walked around the counter and stood by the closed door and listened.

After about five minutes of listening, Jacobs

thought he detected a few sounds, but definitely not anyone's voice. They were faint, but sounded like someone was putting boxes away. He still couldn't be sure of whether somebody was actually in there or not. Maybe there was just one person who was busy working. If there were more than that, they definitely weren't talking to each other. Jacobs didn't want to take too much longer in case the man he just punched out came to his senses again, or if someone else walked through the front door. That would lead to a new host of problems.

Jacobs put his hand on the knob of the door and slowly turned it to see if it was locked. It wasn't. He took out his gun and slowly pushed the door open, ready to fire immediately if need be. There was a man to his right, sitting in a chair, reading a magazine. He wasn't paying any attention to Jacobs. The man saw the door opening out of the corner of his eye, but assumed it was one of their partners, like usual. Jacobs pointed his gun at him, waiting to be acknowledged. After a minute of Jacobs just standing there, the man finally picked his head out of the magazine and looked over. He was stunned, but didn't say a word. With his gun pointed at him, Jacobs motioned with his weapon for the man to get to his feet and move to the back.

There was another man behind the door, oblivious to what was going on. He was putting a few things away and starting to get a little annoyed that the door was still open.

"You gonna keep that thing open all day?" the man asked.

Without getting a reply, he stopped what he was doing to check on why the door was open and nobody was saying or doing anything. He was in for a surprise when he almost got jabbed in the stomach with the barrel of Jacobs' gun.

"Who the hell are you?"

"Police," Jacobs said.

"What the hell are you doing here?"

"I heard you guys had guns in here. That's against the law, you know."

"Where's Ben?"

"Oh, if you're referring to the guy out front, he's taking a little nap."

"You can't just barge in like this."

Jacobs smiled. "Well, looks like I'm here."

"I'll have your badge for this."

"Too late. Already threw it away."

Jacobs motioned with his gun for him to stand over by the wall with his buddy. Jacobs closed the door behind him and stepped further into the room. He would have asked about where they stashed guns, but he didn't have to. There was a table to his left with what was probably two dozen types of weapons. Assault rifles, handguns, ammunition, it was all there.

"Yo, where's your warrant, cop?"

"Don't have one," Jacobs answered.

"You can't arrest us."

"Who said anything about arresting you? I'm just gonna take your guns."

"What? You can't do that?"

"Wanna call a cop?" Jacobs said with a smile. "Maybe you should file a formal complaint and tell them how a police officer came in here and took your illegal weapons away from you."

The man sighed and shook his head. "Unbelievable. This ain't right. And they say we're worse than the cops? That's just downright dirty, man."

"My heart bleeds for your pain."

Jacobs saw several types of duffel bags and started placing the guns and ammunition inside, while still keeping a close look at the two men against the wall. He knew they weren't too happy about him taking their stuff and wouldn't have been surprised if one of them made a move to stop him. Jacobs' movements were interrupted, though, as he heard the handle of the door turning. He scurried behind it as it opened, just in time to see who it was. The man he'd already knocked out once.

"Hey, did you guys see some cop in here?"

Jacobs pounced from behind the door, nailing the man in the back of the head with his gun. The man instantly fell to the floor, knocked out once again. Jacobs looked at him and shook his head.

"Looks like today just ain't your day."

Jacobs went back to the table and finished stuffing the bags until they were full. He threw a bag over each shoulder and looked over at the two men, who were just watching him. They were surprisingly quiet and reserved.

"Either of you two gonna try and stop me or anything?" Jacobs asked.

"Looks like you got all the power right now. But we'll remember this."

"I'm sure you will."

"Cop or no cop. You'll pay for this. You'll be hearing from us again."

"I'm sure of it. I'll be waiting."

Jacobs then walked toward the door, but suddenly stopped as he noticed some boxes sitting on shelves against the wall. He then took a quick look at the men against the wall, before putting the bags down.

"What's in these?" Jacobs asked, pointing to the boxes.

"Just supplies, man. It's nothing."

"Hmm."

Jacobs didn't take him at his word. He wasn't sure what was in the boxes, but it seemed a little out of place with the rest of the room. Maybe it was something he could use, he thought. He grabbed a few boxes off the shelf and sat them on the table. He flicked the lids off them as he looked inside. His face lit up and smiled as he looked up at the men against the wall. The one man was just shaking his head, looking up at the ceiling, seemingly in disbelief that all this was happening.

Jacobs reached into the boxes and pulled out rolls of money, kept together by rubber bands. Bills upon bills, rolled up.

"This real or counterfeit?" Jacobs asked.

"We don't deal in counterfeit, man."

"Well, I'm assuming this was obtained through illegal means so I'm gonna have to confiscate it from you."

"Enjoying yourself?"

"A little bit."

"You should. It won't last long."

"You should know threatening a police officer is a punishable offense," Jacobs said. "Since you're being so nice, though, I'll let you off with just a warning."

The man couldn't help but smile and laugh at the audacity of the man standing before him, taking his guns, stealing his money. But he knew they'd see each other again sometime. Jacobs put the rolls of money in the bags and went back to the shelf to remove more boxes from it. A few of them had more money inside, though some just had ammunition and others had paperwork.

"So how much money's in here?" Jacobs asked.

"I'm assuming you can count. You count it."

Jacobs smiled. "I'll do that."

After putting the rest of the money in the bags, he picked them up and slung them over his shoulders. He'd gotten more than what he was looking for. Worried about them following him after he left, he wanted to make sure that didn't happen. Jacobs looked around and saw the bathroom. That would have to do.

"All right, you two, into the bathroom."

"What?"

"Well, I'm gonna leave now and I don't want you to follow me," Jacobs sarcastically explained. "So, I'm gonna shove you in the bathroom and leave you in there."

The men looked at each other, not liking it one bit. Jacobs tried to alleviate their concerns.

"Don't worry. Your buddy here can let you out when he wakes up."

Though the men were pissed, they still complied with Jacobs' wishes. Jacobs still wasn't sure whether they might try something, so he made sure to give them plenty of room as they went into the bathroom. Once in there, he had them close the door. He looked around for something to put in front of the door and saw a desk that he pushed over in front of it. Knowing they could still climb over or under it, Jacobs sought a few more things he could cover the door with to make their trek a little more difficult. He saw some folding chairs that he intertwined with the desk to make knocking them off not so easy. That would have to do, he thought. He couldn't stay there all day. For all he knew, more of them were on their way.

Jacobs left the storeroom and went back into the front of the store. He closed the door that led into the back and also moved some things in front of the door.

He figured that was enough to slow them down significantly, where they wouldn't be able to catch up with him. He then rushed out of the store, bags draped over both shoulders as he walked down the street to his car. Once in his car, he peeled out of the area as quickly as possible before anybody made him.

Once back at his house, he could hardly believe what he'd just done. He threw his badge away and stole guns and money from a gang like it was nothing. He felt better than he thought he would. He was convinced this was the right thing to do to get justice and revenge for his family. His mind was made up and he wouldn't feel sorry for it. He sat on his couch with the bags on each side of him. Curious about how much money was in there, he opened the bags and removed every roll of cash that he had. He took the rubber band off a roll and started counting. They were hundred-dollar bills. Ten of them. He started counting another one. It was the same. He noticed some of the bills were twenties and not hundreds. He started counting that stack. There were fifty bills in it. He counted a few more to make sure they all followed the same pattern. They did. Every roll of cash was exactly one thousand dollars. Jacobs couldn't believe it. He had fifty rolls. Fifty-thousand dollars.

Jacobs was never one who was inspired much by money. It was a necessary evil as far as he was concerned. Now was no different. He didn't care about having that much money, but he knew that would carry his personal vendetta a lot further. He could use it to pay off informants, get equipment that he needed, or anything else that came up along the way that he could use to get closer to his intended goal. And he would use everything at his disposal to accomplish that task.

7

JACOBS WOKE up by the sound of his phone ringing a little after nine. It was going off the hook. He got up and grabbed it from off the table and looked at it. Buchanan, Captain Whitaker, along with a few other officers, had all tried calling him. He was supposed to have been at work over an hour ago. But he had no intention of going in. He didn't set his alarm the previous night. He wasn't answering his phone. He wasn't taking calls from anyone. As far as he was concerned, that part of his life was over.

As he got himself dressed, he thought it was kind of funny. He actually felt good. It was the best night of sleep he'd had since his family's tragedy. His head felt clearer, he felt more rejuvenated, more energy. It felt like he had a purpose again. He actually ate breakfast for once, something he hadn't done in weeks. He hadn't had much of an appetite since his family was murdered. But suddenly, he almost felt like a new man. He felt like he was unrestricted now. He wasn't worried about a job, or pleasing other people, or trying to act a certain way, or trying to bottle his feelings up inside. Now he felt free. Free to do what he felt was best, without trying to fit it within the confines of the law.

Jacobs was still at his house an hour later, getting ready for the day. He was on the computer researching Mallette's Maulers, trying to get a fix on where they were located. He knew some of their locations from when he was working undercover, but they'd closed up shop and moved operations since then. It was like he had to start from scratch again. His work was interrupted when he heard a knock on the door. Since he wasn't expecting someone, he worried that it might have been someone from the gang that he robbed the day before. Though he figured they probably wouldn't knock upon finding out where he lived, you never know what kind of plans those people had. He looked out the window and saw Buchanan. He knew what the sergeant was doing there. He was there to bring him into work. Jacobs wasn't interested in continuing that same old song and dance. He was through. And he wanted it to remain that way. He let Buchanan knock several times. Jacobs wasn't going to answer. No matter what.

After standing by the door for close to ten minutes, Buchanan finally left. The sergeant didn't know whether Jacobs was actually there or not. His car was there. But maybe he went somewhere without it. Or, maybe he just didn't want to be bothered. In either case, Buchanan had tried. But he knew there was only so much he could do. He could only try to protect his friend, along with his job, for so long. Eventually, he figured Jacobs would have to want it as much as he did for him. And that just didn't seem like it was going to happen.

As Jacobs watched Buchanan go back to his car, he felt a little bad not answering the door for him. Buchanan was a good man. Jacobs knew he genuinely wanted the best for him. But if he talked to him now, all Buchanan would do is try to convince him to come back to work. To let everything be handled by the law. And that just wasn't good enough. Not anymore. Jacobs wasn't interested in having that conversation again.

His phone rang constantly for the next several hours, but Jacobs still didn't pick up. His decision was made, and it did nobody any good to keep rehashing it. He listened to the voicemails, though only for a few seconds, just long enough to either get a name or until he recognized the voice. Once he knew it was someone from the department, he quickly deleted it. Then, a number called that he didn't recognize. He still didn't answer it, thinking it may have been one of the other officers trying to disguise where they were calling from. Jacobs let it go to voicemail, then listened to the message. It wasn't another police officer. It was Franks. It was a brief message, just telling him to call back when he got it. With a certain excitement, Jacobs instantly returned the call.

"Hey, it's Brett Jacobs."

"Hey, good to hear from you," Franks said.

"Sorry I missed your call earlier, I haven't been answering the phone. People been calling me all day wondering why I haven't shown up to work."

Franks laughed it off. "No sweat, man, no sweat. It's all good. Just wanted to let you know everything's a go for today if you can make it."

"What's a go?"

"Got you a meeting with one of my contacts. He can set you up with fake IDs and the like. Just warning you, though, he ain't cheap."

"What's it gonna set me back?" Jacobs asked.

"Depends on how much work you need. I told him your situation, and because he feels good for your cause, he'll give you a discount."

"Which is?"

"He'll give you the basic package for five thousand."

"Five thousand?"

"Yeah. Can you scrounge that up?" Franks asked.

"Yeah, I've got it."

"Tonight good for you?"

"Just name the time."

"Make it seven."

"I'll be there."

"Oh, and by the way, I heard Harry's Dry Cleaning

got taken to the cleaners, so to speak, yesterday," Franks said with a laugh. "Good stuff, man. Couldn't have happened to a nicer bunch of guys. I guess I don't have to ask who was responsible for that."

"How'd you hear about it?"

"One of their boys came into the store and asked me if I knew anything about the guy who did it to them."

"Tell them anything?"

"Hell no, man, ef them pricks. I wouldn't give them directions to the bathroom. They are pretty pissed, though. You'll be having to deal with them again somewhere down the line."

"Can't wait."

"All right, well, I'm closing the store at seven tonight, so meet me here then."

"I'll be there."

Jacobs spent the rest of the day continuing his research into locations of where Mallette's crew might be. He wound up with a few places he could check out, but no definite leads. He also turned his phone off, not wanting to be bothered with the sound of it incessantly ringing. He kept an eye on the time, not wanting to miss his appointment. Once six o'clock rolled around, he shut everything down and made his way to the pawn shop. By the time he got there, he was actually five minutes early. Once Franks saw him enter the store, he rushed over to the door and closed it. He locked the door, pulled down the shade, and turned the open sign to closed.

"So, we already started everything in the back," Franks said, patting Jacobs on the shoulder.

"Who's we?"

"Me and Sang."

"Sang."

"Sang Lee. Best forger in the city. He can make anything and make it look like the real thing. Trust me, there's nobody better."

Jacobs nodded, not really having anything to add. Franks led him to a door behind the counter which led to a back office. Lee was already sitting inside, working. Since he looked like he was concentrating deeply on his work, Franks skipped the introductions.

"He started working on this stuff when I called you earlier and you gave the go-ahead," Franks said.

"Oh."

"Should be almost finished."

They stood there patiently, quietly, as Lee finished up his work. After a few minutes, Lee lifted his head and looked at the two men.

"I assume you have the money," Lee said.

Jacobs reached into his back pocket and removed an envelope. He put it on the desk. Lee picked it up and quickly peeked at the contents, but didn't count it as he assumed it was all there. A smile came over his face.

"Very good. Very good. I am almost done. Just have to finish the driver's license."

Jacobs and Franks just looked at each other and shrugged.

Lee pushed a few other papers to the front of the desk. "Here, you can start looking these over to make sure it meets with your approval."

Jacobs picked the papers up and started looking through them. It was everything he could have possibly needed. Social security number, birth certificate, passports, nothing was left to spare. After a couple more minutes, Lee handed him the driver's license. On all the documents, Jacobs' name had been changed.

"Brian Jackson?" Jacobs asked.

"Yes. Whether you want to use that name in your day-to-day activities, that is up to you," Lee said. "But when any of these documents need to be presented, that is what you'll use."

"And they'll all go through without a hitch?"

"Like clockwork."

"Like I said, man, Sang's the best there is," Franks said.

"Well, thanks. Seems like five-thousand's a little cheap for all this."

Lee tilted his head, agreeing that was the case. "Well, when Eddie told me your story, I thought I would do what I could for you."

"Why's that?"

"I do not like Rich Mallette or his men," Lee plainly stated. "I have done business with them before and I never have much cared for it. An arrogant and obnoxious bunch of hooligans. I try to limit my associations and business with them as much as I can. As a matter of fact, I do believe if I wasn't as good at what I do, they probably would've had me killed off a long time ago. Plus, I heard about what they did to your family. I wish you luck in your endeavor."

Jacobs looked at him and nodded. "Thank you."

"You know, I was thinking," Franks said. "You may wanna do something about your car."

"My car?"

"Yeah. You might wanna either get a new one, or disguise the one you got. Give it a new paint job or something."

"Eddie is correct," Lee said. "Pretty soon, they'll be on the lookout for your vehicle."

"So, what do you suggest?" Jacobs asked.

"Either paint it and get a new license plate or just ditch it entirely," Franks answered. "Plus, all your cop friends know your car. You don't want them to be able to easily spot you by picking up your ride."

"So, what's easier?"

"Honestly, it's probably better to just ditch it all together. I can getcha a new one by tomorrow if you want."

"What's it gonna cost me?"

"Depends. How old's your car now?"

"I dunno. About eight years, I guess," Jacobs said.

"How many miles."

"About a hundred thousand."

"Gimme about two grand," Franks said. "I'll get you another car that can't be traced back to you. Even if a cop's behind you at an intersection and he's running your plates, you'll have nothing to worry about."

"Well, I don't have the money on me."

Franks put his hands up, indicating it wasn't a problem. "No biggie, just bring it with you tomorrow."

"All right."

"Just make sure you clear out everything in the car you wanna keep. 'Cause after tomorrow it'll be going to the chop shop and there ain't no turning back after that."

"You're not gonna get me some beat up looking old station wagon or something, are you?" Jacobs asked.

"What? No way, I'll get you something nice. Won't be brand new, but it'll have less miles than what you got now. I mean, wouldn't do any good to get something new anyway, right?"

"Why?"

"Well, by the looks of what you're aiming to do, why get something new if it might wind up getting shot to pieces anyway?"

"Good point."

"I'll call you tomorrow when I have everything ready."

"OK. Will we be meeting here again?"

"Nah. Can't fit a car in here," Franks joked, then laughed.

Jacobs also managed to crack a smile and a small laugh. "Just let me know where. I'll be there."

"Oh, and just to let you know, Cedeno and his boys are putting out feelers to find out who you are."

Jacobs scrunched his eyebrows together, not knowing who he was talking about. "Cedeno?"

"You know, Harry's?"

"Oh. So?"

"Well, just figured I'd let you know. I give them a few days until they find out who you are. Just giving you the heads-up. Don't be surprised if they wind up on your doorstep one night."

"I'll keep an eye out. Thanks. Mr. Lee? Thanks for these," Jacobs said, holding the documents up.

"Please, call me Sang. And it was my pleasure. You ever have need for my services again, you let me know. You can contact me through Eddie."

"Will do."

Jacobs didn't like the fact that he was going to have to keep looking over his shoulder, wondering when Cedeno's crew was going to find him. Part of him thought about taking the fight to them. If they wanted him, he'd make himself plainly available. Might as well get it over with, he thought. After putting his new forged documents in his pocket, Jacobs walked out of the back office, followed by Franks. Once they got to the door, Jacobs stopped and turned around.

"You really think they'll be able to find me?"

After some brief thought, Franks answered. "Yeah, they got some contacts themselves. I mean, they're not on my level, or on Mallette's or anything, but they're not a bunch of bozos you can dismiss outright either. And trust me, after what you did to them yesterday, they're gonna pull out all the stops in looking for you."

"I don't like waiting. Maybe I should just pay them another visit."

"You serious?"

"Why not? If they're looking for me, maybe I should let them find me," Jacobs said.

"Just so you know, the next time they see you, they're gonna shoot first, talk after."

"Kinda figured."

"So if you walk into that place again, you better be armed, and armed heavy."

Jacobs smiled. "Well, luckily that won't be a problem."

Franks returned the smile. "You know, there's something crazy about you that I like."

"How many men are in that gang?"

Franks shook his head as he thought. "I dunno. Maybe twenty."

"There were only three there yesterday."

"Yeah, usually no more than five there at a time, unless Cedeno's got some big meeting or something."

"Was he there yesterday? Cedeno?" Jacobs asked.

"Yeah, man, he was one of the ones you stuck in the

bathroom. You made him look foolish; he's not forgetting you anytime soon."

Jacobs left the pawn shop and went back to his car. Not wanting to carry a gun in plain sight up the street, he drove down to the dry-cleaning store, parking just in front. He grabbed an assault rifle out of the bag and held it close to his chest, covering it with his jacket. He went into the store, figuring he was about to get an explosive greeting. Upon entering, he saw the same man at the front counter that he knocked out the last time he was there. Once again, the man had his head stuck in a magazine and was barely paying attention when he walked in.

"Hey there," Jacobs said. "Remember me?"

The man didn't say a word, but quickly tossed down his magazine and started lunging for something underneath the counter. He wasn't going to let the cop do the same thing to him again. Jacobs could only assume that the man was reaching for some sort of weapon. He let his jacket fly open and he removed the assault rifle, pointing it at the man in case his suspicions were right. As soon as the man straightened up, Jacobs saw the rifle in his hands. He wasn't going to let the other guy shoot first. Jacobs immediately fired, several bullets ripping into the man's body, sending him flying backward.

Almost immediately, the back door swung open, with another man looking out, curious at what all the commotion was about. Upon seeing his dead friend on the floor, he glanced up and saw Jacobs with a gun in his hands and assumed they were being hit by a rival gang. He grabbed a pistol from his belt and aimed for him, but Jacobs already had him beat. A few seconds later, the man was down on the floor, joining his friend in the afterlife.

Jacobs walked around the counter to the back door, seeing if there were any other surprises there for him. He took a peek inside and almost got his head blown off, bullets missing him by inches. Knowing he was likely to get shot as soon as he stepped inside, he looked for a diversion. He saw a red piece of fabric on the counter and grabbed it. He threw it in the room, drawing gunfire from whoever was inside. As soon as the gun stopped firing, Jacobs surged through the door, firing in the direction the bullets were coming from. At first, he heard the man groaning. Then, he saw the man slump to the floor. Jacobs was on his guard, knowing there might be more somewhere. He took a look around the room, but the place seemed empty. After making sure that it was, Jacobs went back to each of the three victims to get a better look at their faces. None were Cedeno.

The whole incident turned out to be an epic fail in Jacobs' mind. He didn't go in there just to kill people. He went in there because he knew Cedeno wanted revenge, and he'd eventually surprise Jacobs some-where down the line. Jacobs was trying to avoid all that and get it over with as quickly as possible. Now, he still had to worry about the same thing. Cedeno would obviously still be looking for payback. Before leaving, Jacobs noticed a few security cameras set up along the top of the walls. There were several in the back room and a couple in the front of the store. Jacobs took his weapon and shot every single one of them, crushing them to pieces. Cedeno may well yet find out he was there, but he wouldn't be able to see it personally.

It was the first time that Jacobs had ever killed anyone. Even in all his years with the police, he never even fired his gun before. Though he felt a small sense of sadness come over him, Jacobs knew he didn't have time to worry about it. Assuming that someone nearby would have heard all the shots being fired and called the police, Jacobs knew he had to go. He rushed out of the store and sped out of the area before any of his former friends got there.

The transformation had begun. From a family man and hard-working cop to a take no prisoners vigilante hell-bent on getting his own brand of justice. And this was just the beginning.

8

THE FOLLOWING MORNING, Jacobs woke up to the sound of banging on his door. As he moved into the living room, he heard a constant barrage of knocks by some heavy-handed individual, as well as someone hollering at the same time. Assuming Cedeno wouldn't have given him the courtesy of knocking, he looked through the peephole to see who it was.

"I know you're in there, Brett," Buchanan yelled. "Sooner or later you're gonna have to open the door and face me."

Jacobs rolled his eyes and sighed, not really wanting to deal with it at the moment. He stood there for a few minutes, wondering what he should do. He didn't really want to open it and talk to him. But it also seemed like he wasn't going away. The knocking persisted for several more minutes.

"I'm not going anywhere, Brett, until you open this door. Your car's out front, I know you're there."

Franks was right. He really did need to get a new vehicle so nobody could spot him. After another couple minutes of self-deliberation, Jacobs finally decided to open the door.

"Planning on busting it down soon?" Jacobs asked.

"It crossed my mind."

Buchanan walked past his friend, though he wasn't invited to come in. Jacobs didn't look pleased that his friend just barged right in. Jacobs forcefully shut the door. Buchanan walked around the living room in a circle, as if he was inspecting the place.

"Missed you at work yesterday," Buchanan said. "And today."

Jacobs looked at the time and saw it was just about ten o'clock. He didn't respond. He didn't have anything to say.

"Looks like they're putting you on suspension for the time being."

"Doesn't matter," Jacobs said.

"Why? Why are you doing this? You're throwing your career away? Your pension? And for what? So you can sit around and sulk all day?"

"That's not what I'm doing."

"Then what? Why are you doing this?"

"It's better if you don't know."

Buchanan took a step back and raised one of his eyebrows as he thought he understood what was being implied. "You're not planning on doing things your own way, are you?"

"Somebody's got to."

"Brett, put aside all this nonsense that you're thinking and come back to work. Let them know you still want the job, take the couple weeks' suspension, and get on with your life again."

"I am getting on with my life," Jacobs said. "Maybe it's not the way that you want, but I'm doing what I think I need to do. Being a cop doesn't interest me anymore."

"You know what you're saying?"

"I've already thought about it. Maybe this is what you were meant to do, but it's not for me."

Buchanan looked disappointed, but could tell that Jacobs' mind was made up and he wasn't going to be able to change it. He nodded as he started walking around the room again, still having an unpleasant look on his face. "So, have you given thought to what you're going to be doing then?"

"Yeah."

"Mind sharing?"

"Maybe I'll become a bounty hunter, or a private detective, or a security guard, or a bodyguard, I dunno, something where I can make sure people get what's coming to them."

Once again, Buchanan didn't quite like the sound of that. There were too many little references to Jacobs taking the law into his own hands for his liking. As he paced around the room, something clicked in his head. He didn't want to believe it, but he now had to ask.

"Did, uh, you hear about the shooting last night?" Buchanan asked.

Jacobs shook his head. "No, what shooting? I was here all night."

"Some dry-cleaning store got lit up. Found three dead bodies inside."

"Oh. That's terrible. Some kind of robbery?"

"We don't think so. All three were gang members. They belong to Ronnie Cedeno's crew."

"Oh. Hadn't heard. Probably retaliation of some sort."

"Yeah, probably. Funny thing about that," Buchanan said, still pacing. "We found an eyewitness who happened to be walking on the street around the same time."

"Oh. Well, that's good for you."

"Yeah. She said it was just one man. Only one man came out of the store after the sound of the shots."

"Is that right?" Jacobs asked, keeping up the charade.

"Yeah. Just one man. You know, it didn't hit me until just now."

"What's that?"

"The description. The description of the man she gave... fits you to a T."

"Oh yeah? Wow, some coincidence."

"Isn't it?"

"Was she able to get the car this person drove away in?"

"No, just that it was a dark-colored car."

"Oh, that's too bad. Well, maybe there's some video or something you could use," Jacobs said.

"Security cameras were in the store but they were all shot to pieces. Nothing usable."

"Looks like you got your work cut out for you. Probably just a gang hit, though."

"Yeah, probably. You didn't happen to be in that area last night?"

"Me? No. Like I said, I was here all night."

"Good. Just figured I'd ask. You did fit the description."

"What possible reason would I have for doing that?"

"I don't know," Buchanan said. "Your reasons for doing a lot of the things seem to escape me. This wouldn't seem to be much different."

Jacobs didn't want to stand there and rehash what happened the night before just in case he let something slip out. And there was nothing else for them to talk about, so he tried to usher his friend along.

"Well, sorry to cut this short, but I have some things I have to do today," Jacobs said, walking over to the door.

"Such as?"

"Looking for people. Work, that is. Gotta get the ball rolling, right?"

The Fallen

Buchanan walked to the door as well, afraid of what his friend was intending to do, but knowing there really wasn't anything he could do to stop it. He walked out the door, but before leaving, he turned back to give some last-minute advice.

"You be careful out there."

"Always," Jacobs said confidently.

"Just make sure you don't get in too much over your head."

"I won't."

"And I sure hope we never meet again under more unpleasant circumstances."

"Nothing could ever be more unpleasant than meeting over the death of my family."

Buchanan nodded, knowing the rage of that tragedy was still consuming Jacobs, still flowing through his veins. But he knew he'd done all he could. The rest was up to Jacobs. Buchanan had an idea what Jacobs was planning on doing. He just hoped he wouldn't have to be the one arresting him when the time came. As he went back to his car, Jacobs kept an eye on him through the window, just to make sure he actually left.

Once Jacobs saw the car leave, he made himself breakfast, then got back to the computer, continuing his search for Mallette's crew. Most of what he was coming up with was information that he already knew or had been checked out when he was actually working in law enforcement. And most of that information was now outdated. But there was something that was new, something that he hadn't seen before. It was an address that was owned by Rich Mallette, one that either got overlooked by investigators when they were putting the package together of everything owned under the Mallette corporate umbrella, or it was brand new. If it was something that just got overlooked and should've been written down before, it was likely it would turn out to be a dead end. They probably would have moved shop from there. But if it was new, maybe it was the thing he needed to get his crusade moving. In either case, it was a place to start.

Within twenty minutes, Jacobs had gotten himself together and left his house to investigate the new address. While not wanting to get too excited about what he may or may not find, he was still hopeful. When he finally got to his destination, that hope had waned. It appeared to be an old abandoned warehouse. Jacobs got out of his car and stood on the perimeter of the property, which had a steel fence encompassing it, along with a gate in front, which had a gate chain and padlock keeping them from opening. Jacobs stood there, staring at the building, looking for a sign that the place was actually in use. There wasn't a car in sight. But that wasn't going to stop Jacobs from looking into it further.

Jacobs went back to his car and into the bag of weapons that he'd previously confiscated from Cedeno. He remembered seeing a pair of hand-held bolt cutters in there. He imagined that they'd probably broken through a few locked doors while in Cedeno's possession, not that it really concerned him now. He was just thankful that it was in there. Jacobs went back to the gate and took a quick look around to make sure nobody was walking along the road or that a car was driving by. The warehouse was not in a heavily populated or trafficked area, so the coast was clear. Jacobs cut through the chain with the bolt cutters and he pushed the gates open. He got back in his car and drove the rest of the way up to the warehouse, parking in front of what he assumed to be the office area doors.

Jacobs pulled on the glass doors, but just like the front gate, they were locked. And just like the front gate, that wasn't going to stop him. He looked through the window, but still didn't see any signs of activity. He went back to the car and pulled out the bolt cutters again and drove them right through the glass door, shattering it into pieces. He stepped through the newly opened door, not even bothering to unlock it and enter the normal way. Just in case he ran into trouble, he removed his gun and kept it firmly gripped in his hand. As he maneuvered through the office, checking out several rooms, he searched for anything that might have been left behind. A scrap of paper, an invoice, a list of names, anything that he could use in his quest. After a half hour of looking, he came up with nothing. It was remarkably clean. Whoever was there beforehand took great care in making sure nothing was left behind. Once he was done with the office area, Jacobs took a look into the warehouse, but it was just more of the same. Dejected, he went back to his car. Almost immediately after getting in, his phone rang.

"Yeah?"

"Hey, just wanted to let you know I got your new wheels," Franks said.

"Good. Name the time and I'll be there."

"Well, can't really do it here. Wouldn't look good switching cars in front of my place of business."

"Since when did you ever get so concerned about how things look?" Jacobs asked.

"Fair point, fair point. Fine. Meet me here in half an hour."

"I'll be there."

Jacobs turned the car on, and was about ready to start driving when he saw a couple cars driving into the property. He was stunned to see one was a marked police car. The other he recognized as belonging to Buchanan. He got out of his car and leaned up against the driver's side door as he waited for his visitors to approach him. The patrol officers got out of their car but stayed close by it. Buchanan was the only one who walked over to him.

"What are you doing here?" Buchanan asked.

Jacobs wasn't too keen on answering any questions. "What are *you* doing here?"

"That's a question I should be asking you, don't you think?"

Jacobs shrugged. "I dunno, is it?"

"Brett, what are you doing?"

"I told you I was getting into some private investigation work. That's what I'm doing."

"You haven't filed any paperwork in regards to that. You know, licenses, and things like that."

"I'll get to it."

"I noticed the front gate looked like it'd been cut open," Buchanan said.

"Yeah, I noticed that too. That's why I came in further. Wanted to make sure no trouble was going on or anything."

Buchanan grinned, knowing he was being fed a bunch of baloney. He looked at the warehouse for a moment and saw the broken glass by the front door. He pointed to it. "And that?"

Jacobs didn't break stride from his story or hesitate at all. "Yeah. Same thing. Came up here, saw the door like that, went in to make sure everything was OK."

"So'd you find what you were looking for inside?"

Jacobs shrugged again, not admitting what he was looking for. "Everything's clean in there. Doesn't look like it's been used for a while."

"Too bad. So, you know who owns this place?"

"Uh, no, no, have no idea."

"Just so happens Rich Mallette is listed as the owner."

"That a fact?" Jacobs asked.

"Quite a coincidence you showing up here at one of his facilities."

"Yeah, it is at that."

"So, what were you hoping to find?"

Jacobs shook his head, taking a second to think of his answer. "I'd gotten a tip that Frazier might have been hiding out here. Wanted to take a look for myself."

"Why didn't you call it in then? We could've come down and checked it out."

"Well, I know how busy things are. Wanted to make sure it was valid first," Jacobs said.

"Or you wanted to take things into your own hands?"

"Just want what's right."

"How 'bout you come down to the station?" Buchanan asked. "The captain wants to talk to you."

Jacobs wasn't going anywhere. He wasn't seeing anyone or talking to anybody. Not unless he was forced to. "Nah. I'm not talking to anybody."

"Brett, he just wants to make a last-ditch effort to save your job."

"Well, he can forget it. I'm not interested in saving it."

"You know I could make you go down there if I really wanted to."

"Is that what they're for?" Jacobs asked, nodding to the other two officers. "Backup?"

"Why are you making this so difficult? So hard on yourself?"

"It's just the way things are, Bucky. It's the way things have to be."

"I think I could bring you down on suspicion of breaking and entering."

"You see me do it?"

"No. But I doubt they would've just left the gate open like that."

"Like I said, that's how I found it."

"Or the door."

"You see anything on me that looks like I broke it?" Jacobs asked.

"No, but I could search the car."

"Probable cause?"

"Or if you're carrying a gun."

Jacobs opened up his jacket and revealed his gun inside. "I was a cop. I'm licensed to carry, you know that. Is that what you wanna do? Play these silly games with me?"

"No, it's not what I want to do," Buchanan said. "But you're beginning to make it very hard for me. You're not being cooperative, you up and left your job without warning, people are starting to think you might be a danger to yourself and others."

"I'm not a danger to myself."

"And others?"

"Depends on what others you're talking about,"

Jacobs said. "If you're talking about a little old lady walking down the street, then no, she's not in any danger. Not from me. Or a bunch of kids playing basketball at the neighborhood court, no, they're not in any danger either."

"And if they so happen to be employed by Rich Mallette?"

"Then I would assume they should be looking over their shoulders. I mean, a lot of bad people out there. With Mallette in jail, there might be people looking to assert their power, take on more territory for themselves. Lot can happen out here."

Buchanan scratched his face as he listened to what he thought was his friend talking crazy. "Or some people might have revenge on their mind and try to do what they think the law isn't?"

Jacobs shrugged. "You never know."

Buchanan knew his conversation was going nowhere, and he sensed he was losing his friend. He put his hand on Jacobs' forearm to try and emphasize his point. "Brett, don't do anything stupid."

Jacobs looked straight into his eyes to let him know he wasn't fooling around and he knew exactly what he was doing. "Stupid left the farm a long time ago."

9

JACOBS GOT to the pawn shop about forty-five minutes after his encounter with Buchanan. He went into the store, which appeared to be empty. There was no sign of Franks. Thinking he might have been in the back office, Jacobs went to the door that led to the back. Just as he put his hand on the knob, the door swung open. Franks jumped back, surprised to see someone standing there in front of him. Seeing that it was Jacobs, he put his hand on his heart and let out a deep breath.

"Don't do that," Franks said, still breathing a bit heavily.

Jacobs grinned. "Sorry. Wasn't sure if you were here."

"Of course I'm here. Where else would I be? Almost gave me a heart attack, man."

"Well, you told me to meet you here."

Franks pulled out his phone and looked at the time. "I also said thirty minutes."

"Had a little bit of a delay."

"Nothing serious, I hope."

"I've got it handled."

"All right, let me close things down for a bit before I show you your new ride," Franks said, walking over to the front door and locking it.

Jacobs noticed he seemed to do that quite frequently. "You seem to do that often. Do you even try to sell anything in here?"

Franks laughed. "You see them breaking down the door to get in here? Besides, this ain't my main gig. Just gives me a good cover. You know how it is."

"You better hope I never go back on the force."

"You kidding? With how friendly we are now, how could you do that to me? Besides, I hear you go back on the force, there'll be a moved sign on that door the same day."

"Well, don't think you'll ever have to worry about that. It's a good thing you convinced me about the car."

"Why?"

"The reason I'm late. I think my former friends and colleagues followed me from my house to an abandoned warehouse that I linked up to Mallette's crew."

A smile came over Franks' face, happy that he was proven to be right. "Ahh, see? I told you. Never doubt the old master here."

"I'll try to remember that."

Franks started walking to the back and waved for Jacobs to come along. "Follow me. Got your new car in the alley out back. Got you an SUV. Figured you could use the extra space for gear and equipment."

"Good idea."

"Yeah. I figured if you're gonna go up against Mallette's Maulers, you're gonna need room for, like, a cache of weapons and stuff. It's only five years old, about sixty-thousand miles, so everything should be good to go."

"Sounds like it should work fine."

"What are your plans after this?"

"Well, I wanna try finding Mallette's bunch, but I think I gotta look for a new place first."

"A new place? You need help with that?"

"You help with moving too?" Jacobs asked.

Franks smiled. "Well, only for my friends, of course."

"And a little fee?"

"Yeah, that too."

"I dunno, I was just planning on finding some shady motel or something somewhere I could lay low for a while."

"You ain't gotta do that. That's still risky. Someone will give you up in those places if they think it helps their situation at all, you know that."

"Don't have many other options at the moment," Jacobs said.

"Yes you do." Franks handed Jacobs the keys to his

new car. "Here, why don't you get whatever you need out of your old car and put them in the new one. While you're doing that, I'll make a call."

"Do you know someone for everything?"

Franks thought for a minute. "Uh, yeah, I think so."

Jacobs went back through the entrance to get to his old car, removing everything that he needed. It didn't take long, though. He only had three bags of stuff in it that he needed. Two bags of guns, weapons, and ammunition, and one bag of money. As he walked back into the shop, one bag slung over each of his shoulders, and carrying the third one, he heard Franks talking on the phone. He only heard bits and pieces of the conversation, but could tell it was about him. After putting the bags in the new car, he just stood in the back alley, leaning up against the hood as he waited for Franks to finish his call. He didn't want to go back in and snoop in on the conversation. He knew these types of things took time to finalize and work out the details. Jacobs thought he might have to wait awhile, but actually only waited about five minutes. Franks came walking out the back door, phone still in his hand, eager to share his news.

"OK. Looks like you're good to go."

Jacobs wasn't sure what he was referring to and looked confused. "Good to go? Go where?"

"Your new place."

"My new place? You wanna wind this back and explain it to me a little more slowly?"

"So, I called my contact and asked if he had any vacancies," Franks answered. "Low and behold, he does. Told him your situation, and he was a little hesitant at first because of your prior employment, but I explained all that and he's good with it."

Jacobs threw his hands up, still not sure what was happening. "And where is it? What am I paying for it? What are the particulars?"

"Oh. Well, the particulars are it's on the north side, a small two bedroom, two bath condo. I think he's charging you like twelve-hundred a month for it. It's not a dump of an area either. You'll like it."

"I wasn't really figuring on living in another house. I mean, that's a lot of upkeep and things like that. I was hoping for something I didn't have to put in much time for maintenance or anything. That's why I figured on a hotel or something."

Franks waved his hand at him. "Nah, this is much better. Think about it. Once the crap starts going down, this vendetta you got going on, you know they're gonna be looking for you."

"Yeah, I know."

"So where do you think they're gonna do that at? Hotels, motels, every seedy little establishment in town. This way, you're renting a condo, won't even be in your name."

"It won't?" Jacobs asked.

"Nope. Remember those little documents our friend drew up for you earlier?"

"Yeah."

"Lease gets signed in that name, you want cable, phone, electric, whatever, you put it in that name," Franks said proudly. "Nobody will ever be the wiser. They'll never find you there. Unless you get chummy with the neighbors and they recognize you and then dime you out. Then it's on you and you're on your own."

"Well, I think we can count out me getting chummy with anybody."

"Great. Perfect fit then. Just need to part with six-thousand before you move in."

"Six-thousand? For what?"

"Well, three months' security deposit, plus a little something for me."

Jacobs looked at him for a minute, thinking, adding the numbers up in his head. "So, you get twenty-four hundred for bringing me in?"

"Well, I gave you a little bit of a discount," Franks said, his voice raised a little, hoping it wasn't an issue.

"You did, huh? From what?"

"Twenty-five hundred."

Jacobs laughed to himself and shook his head. He wasn't upset about the money. Franks had already done a lot for him in the short time they'd known each other, and Jacobs realized he probably stuck his neck out a little in trusting his story as quickly as he did, so he didn't begrudge him taking some money for his own services. Jacobs went into his new car and removed the black duffel bag of money and placed it on the ground. They both knelt beside it as Jacobs grabbed a couple stacks. He removed five rolls and handed it to Franks. Though Franks was appreciative and liked the extra dough, he could tell it was more than he had asked for.

Franks tossed the rolled bills in his hand, getting a feel for them. "This looks like a little more than I bargained for."

"Five thousand," Jacobs plainly said. "For the condo and the car."

"Oh crap, I'd forgotten to even charge you for the car," Franks said with a laugh.

Jacobs couldn't help but let out another laugh. "Does that cover it?"

"Yeah, with a little extra. You still have another five hundred to play with, my friend. I'll put it on your credit."

"I guess I should probably get a new phone."

"Consider it done. I'll get you a new one by tomorrow."

"Thanks. You know, you could've just taken the extra money, I wouldn't have known the difference," Jacobs said.

"Ahh, I'm not out here to gouge anyone. Just looking to do an honest day's work for a fair price."

"An honest day's work?"

"Honest, good, evil, whatever, what's the difference? It all comes down to the same thing. Besides, I figure if

I'm honest with you, treat you right, you'll trust me and come back to me for all your future needs."

"Spoken like a true businessman."

"Hey, that's what it's all about, right? Doing business, making money."

"What makes you think they'll be any part of me still alive after this is all over to do business with?"

Franks shook his head. "I don't. But there's something about you. Something that makes me think you're just crazy enough to make it through all this nonsense. I hope I'm right."

"That makes two of us."

Franks reached into his pocket and removed a piece of paper, handing it to Jacobs. Written down was an address and a phone number.

"What's this?" Jacobs asked.

"Address of your new place."

"You don't happen to have keys to that too, do you?"

Franks laughed. "Don't be silly, of course not."

"And the phone number?"

"Call him when you're ready to go over there. He said anytime today or tomorrow is good for him. Just make sure you got the money with you and he'll hand over the keys."

"This guy is trustworthy?"

"Oh yeah. Yeah. He won't give you up or nothing. You can count on that. This ain't his first rodeo hiding people out. He's like me."

"How's that?"

"He wants the repeat business too," Franks said with a smile. "Oh, and I need your keys to the old wheels."

Jacobs dug into his pocket and handed him the keys. Once Jacobs left the area, he immediately went back to his house to collect the rest of his belongings that he wanted to take with him. It wasn't much, basically clothes, his computers, and a few pictures. Everything else was a painful memory that he didn't want to keep reliving. He was careful to make sure that he wasn't being watched at the house, especially with the new car. He didn't want to give up the surprise of the car an hour after getting it. It took Jacobs less than an hour to pack up and grab everything he wanted to take with him.

After putting all his things in the car, Jacobs sat in front of his house for a few minutes. He looked up at it, wondering if this would be the last time he'd set eyes on it. It was a sad moment for him. He pictured him and Val running up the steps to the front door when they first got the keys after signing the paperwork for it. He quickly erased the images from his mind, knowing he had to keep moving. Then, he thought of his dad. He figured he should probably talk to him, tell him the situation, let him know what was happening so he wouldn't be left wondering why he disappeared.

Jacobs went straight over to his dad's house. Seeing a strange car in the driveway, he almost didn't answer the door when his son knocked. Once the door was opened, Mr. Jacobs gave his son a hug, before anything was even said. A few tears came out of Jacobs' eyes, wondering if his dad already knew what was going on. Once inside, they sat down at the kitchen table. It was a little difficult at first for Jacobs to start, not wanting to disappoint his father with what he was about to tell him. Part of him felt like he was probably letting him down. He cleared his throat a few times before beginning.

"I, uh, I guess I should probably tell you why I'm here."

His father smiled. "Not just to visit I guess, huh?"

Jacobs returned the smile. "No. It's not that simple."

"Does it have anything to do with you quitting your job?"

Jacobs looked at his father, wondering how he knew that. "How'd you...?"

"Bucky's called here a few times."

Jacobs nodded. Now it made sense. "Ahh, good old Bucky."

"He's a good friend. He's been concerned about you."

"Yeah."

"So, what's going on?" Mr. Jacobs asked. "You loved being a police officer. Why are you throwing it all away?"

Jacobs started shaking his head, almost immediately losing control of his emotions. His eyes started tearing up again and he cleared his throat once more.

He was barely able to talk. "Because..." His eyes started dancing throughout the room, not able to focus on anything as he tried to control himself and collect his thoughts. His father placed his hand on top of his son's, trying to help him calm down. Mr. Jacobs could tell it was eating away at him.

"Just breathe, son. Just breathe."

Jacobs did as his father recommended and took a few deep breaths. After a couple of minutes, he was finally able to calm down and get himself under control. Once he did, he wiped the tears from his eyes. When it looked like he was finally himself again, his father tried to take charge of the situation, while still being gentle with his obviously fragile son.

"Now, calmly, just tell me what's going on."

"It's been over a month since... since..."

"I know. I know," Mr. Jacobs said, tapping his son's hand.

"There's no leads, no nothing. They're not gonna find the person who did it. He's underground."

"And if you leave the department, what do you plan on doing?"

"Finding him. Making him pay. Making every single person on Mallette's crew pay," Jacobs said.

"You're talking about doing things outside of the law."

"I have to. I can't sleep. I can't focus. I can't do anything knowing that the people who did this are out there and not paying the price."

Mr. Jacobs could see the pain on his son's face. He also could tell that by quitting his job, there was probably no talking him out of it. It seemed as if he'd already gotten the ball rolling.

"Whose car is that out there?"

"Mine," Jacobs answered. "Just traded it in."

"I guess you've already started on this little crusade of yours, huh?"

"Dad, I'm sorry. I know I'm disappointing you and..."

"Stop right there," Mr. Jacobs said. "You have never, ever been a disappointment to me. No matter what you do or where you go, you will always be my son. And I will always love and support you. No matter what. That won't ever change."

Jacobs wiped his eyes and his nose as he felt himself losing control of his emotions again. He nodded, and after a few seconds, was able to compose himself. "I just wanted to come here and let you know what was happening in case you didn't hear from me for a while."

Mr. Jacobs knew what his son was saying, though it was difficult to hear. "So how long will you be gone?"

"I dunno. It might be some time. If the police come looking for me, they might wind up putting a tail on you or watch the house or something, so I'll have to be extra careful."

"Just make sure that you are."

Then, the front door swung open. Jacobs jumped

out of his chair and removed his gun, pointing it at the intruder. Mr. Jacobs could see how tightly wound his son was at that moment. His other son, Terry, walked through the door, slightly alarmed at seeing his brother pointing a gun at him. Once he saw who it was, Jacobs put the gun away and sat back down.

"Jeez, Brett, who'd you think I was?"

"Sorry," Jacobs said.

Terry sat down at the table with his father and brother. He had a few things on his own mind that he wanted to express.

"You wanna tell me why Bucky's calling me and asking what's going on with you?" Terry asked.

"He must be calling everyone," Jacobs said.

"Did you quit your job?"

Jacobs sighed, not really wanting to get into the detailed explanation again. "It's a long story."

Mr. Jacobs put his hand on Terry's arm to let him know to ease off.

"If you guys could sell the house for me, I'd appreciate it."

"Sell the house? Where are you going?" Terry asked.

"I have to do some things."

"Such as?"

"I don't wanna get into it right now," Jacobs said. "Just, you know, whatever you can get for it. I'll try to check in from time to time to let you know I'm all right."

"Check in?" Terry asked, confused and looking at his father for answers.

"I'm not gonna be able to let you know where I'm at and all, but I'll try to call every now and then."

"What are you doing? Running away from everything? From everyone?"

"No. I'm gonna make sure this ends soon. So nobody else has to go through the pain that I've been going through."

"Are you saying what I think you're saying? What do you intend on doing, killing everyone in your path?"

Jacobs shook his head. "Not everyone. Just those who deserve it."

"Brett, you're talking crazy. This isn't the Wild West. You can't just go out shooting whoever you feel like. You're gonna wind up in a prison cell."

"I know what I'm doing."

"Like hell you do," Terry said, not wanting to let his brother go down the path he seemed to be walking.

Mr. Jacobs stayed quiet as the two brothers argued, knowing there was nothing that could be said or done that would change the mind of the youngest. He could see that Brett was a different man than he was before the tragedy. It was to be expected. Nobody could live through something like that and not wind up different.

"And what about us?" Terry asked. "We're still your family. You're just gonna abandon us all while you go self-destruct and play Wyatt Earp out there?"

"I'm not abandoning anybody. That's why I'm here. To let you know what's happening so you're not left wondering where I am."

"So that's it, huh?"

"I've gotta do this."

"And suppose that you do. What then? Where do you go from here?"

Jacobs shrugged, not thinking that far ahead.

"Just say you are successful in this little vendetta of yours," Terry said. "When it's all over, assuming you're still alive, or not locked up, where do you go? What do you do? You probably won't be able to walk down the middle of the street without hanging a hat over your face so nobody can see you."

"I can't worry about that right now. Just gotta do what's right for the moment. The future will take care of itself."

Terry put his hands over his head, not really believing the conversation was happening. He was frustrated that he couldn't make any headway getting through to his brother. For Jacobs, there was really nothing else that needed to be said. His mind was made up, and wheels had already been set in motion, so there was no turning back now anyway. Not that he wanted to. He pushed his chair out, ready to be on his way.

"Well, I should be going," Jacobs said. "I don't wanna stay in one spot for too long."

His father and brother pushed their chairs out as

well, each of them giving him a farewell hug. They all hoped it wouldn't be the last time they would see each other.

"You be careful," Mr. Jacobs said.

Jacobs nodded, looking at both of them one last time, hoping it wouldn't be final. As he left, Terry looked at his father, not believing what just happened. He thought they could've done more to stop him.

"Why didn't you knock some sense into him?" Terry asked.

"He's a broken man. You can see it in his face. He needs closure. He needs peace. Maybe this is the only way he'll find it."

Terry wasn't sure that was the case, but he seemed a little more at ease with the answer. "I just hope he knows what he's doing."

"So do I."

"What if he ends up next to Val and the kids?"

"Somehow, I don't think that's something he'd object to."

"You're just giving up on him?"

"No. I would never. You know that," Mr. Jacobs said. "But with all he's been through, he needs support. And he needs it from us. As much as we can give him, whether we agree with what he's doing or not."

"I guess."

"Who's to say we would act differently if we were in his shoes?"

"I just don't wanna lose him too."

"Then we'll make sure if he ever needs help from us, that we give it to him."

"I wish there was more we could do to help him. To stop him from going down this path," Terry said.

"That's something I don't think is possible. He needs to put this behind him somehow."

"Maybe. He just... seems so different. He had a different kind of look in his eyes."

"Because there's a different man in there. That's not the same Brett we used to know. He died a month ago."

10

JACOBS WAS SITTING in front of the condo he was supposed to be renting, waiting for the owner. He'd called the man a few hours earlier and agreed to meet at ten o'clock. Jacobs wanted to wait until after darkness had set in to disguise his movements somewhat. A couple minutes after ten, he saw a man walking along the pathway that led to the door. Jacobs quickly got out of his car and soon joined him.

"You the man?"

"If you own this house, then I am," Jacobs said.

"Well, yeah, I am."

"You got a name?"

"Call me Broxton."

"That a first name or last name?"

"Either. That's all my tenants need to know. The less we know about each other the better. Don't care what you do, as long as you pay me on time and you don't damage the place. Other than that, do whatever you like."

"Works for me."

Broxton then turned and walked over to the door, unlocking it. Once inside, he flicked on a light switch. To Jacobs' surprise, it didn't look too bad. He half expected trash on the ground, torn up furniture, and graffiti on the walls. Luckily, none of those things were present. It wasn't lavishly furnished, but it had the basics, which was good enough. He hated the thought of getting furniture for it and actually moving his stuff. All that would do is take time away from his main business.

"What do you think of it?" Broxton asked.

Jacobs looked around the main room. "Not bad. Didn't think it'd be furnished already."

"Well, it ain't the Taj Mahal, but it works, right? If you wanna bring in your own stuff, feel free."

"This should work. All I need's the basics."

"Great, then you're all set," Broxton said, handing over the keys to the place.

"There something I need to sign?"

"Nope. I don't do contracts or anything. Just a mess of paperwork that I don't have the time or patience for. Just hand me the money and we're all square."

Jacobs reached into his pocket and removed an envelope, handing it to him. Broxton opened it and saw a large amount of cash. It looked like more than what he required. He quickly ran his fingers through the bills and counted.

"Little bit more here than I asked for."

"Six months in advance," Jacobs said. "Figured it was better for both of us."

"Hey, works for me."

With everything settled, Broxton left, leaving Jacobs to walk around his new place for a few minutes, getting the feel of it. It felt strange to him, being there in a different house, knowing this was where he would be staying for a considerable amount of time. Once he was done checking the place over, he went back to his car and brought in his stuff. After he got everything set up, he crashed on the couch and fell asleep.

When Jacobs woke up the next morning, he went to the neighborhood convenience store and picked up some things for his refrigerator. Once he was settled, he sat down at the kitchen table and went on his laptop, trying to find any clues that would lead to the whereabouts of Lucky Frazier or the rest of Mallette's Maulers. He knew they were out there somewhere. They'd been remarkably silent over the past month, almost like they'd skipped town. But Jacobs knew that wasn't the case. They were just waiting for the right moment to show their faces again. Once they did, that would make them much easier to track down. Trouble was, there was no way of telling how long that would take. And Jacobs' patience wasn't at an all-time high at the moment.

After not coming up with much, Jacobs called the one person he thought might have some type of lead. The one person who seemed to know something about everything. Eddie Franks was quickly becoming Jacobs' go-to person for everything.

"Hey, how you liking your new digs, man?"

"Just swell," Jacobs said. "Wondering if you could do me a favor?"

"Sure, name it."

"You know I'm looking for Mallette's crew."

"Sure do."

"I'm not sure if you're aware of this, but Lucky Frazier is the one who actually killed my family. Him and one other guy that was never identified."

"Yeah?" Franks hesitantly said, afraid he knew where this was heading.

"I'm having trouble locating these guys. They all seem to have run for cover. Any ideas where they might be?"

"Why come to me with this, man? Don't you still have police contacts or something?"

"I gave up my police contacts."

"You trying to get me killed or something? They find out I freely handed out information to someone about them and they'll have my neck."

"Well, that pretty much tells me that you know something," Jacobs said.

"Aww, c'mon, man. I thought we were becoming friends?"

"We are. That's why I'm coming to you."

"I have a feeling you're going to become the bane of my existence."

"We all have one. I give you my word, nobody will ever know it came from you. In fact, I'll do one better, I'll make it known it came from that creep Cedeno."

Franks laughed. "All right, all right, now I can dig it. OK, I don't know exactly where any of them are. But I know they liked to frequent a certain massage parlor, where you got more than just massages, if you catch my meaning. You know, like, wink, wink."

"I get the meaning."

"Yeah, well, anyway, I've heard there's a couple of girls there named Lucy and Deb, and that they were favorites of a couple of the guys. One of which may or may not be a man with a certain nickname we both know."

"You afraid your phone's tapped or something?" Jacobs asked. "Why can't you just come out and say something without dancing around it."

"Hey, you never know who might be listening. I've learned it's best to say something without really saying it, if you know what I mean."

"All right, I'll check this place out. What's the address?"

Franks then gave him the name of it, along with the address. "Listen, if you go there, at the main desk, you wanna ask for a number five."

"A number five?"

"Yeah. That lets them know what you're there for."

"It does?"

"Yeah. I believe they'll lead you into a back room that's reserved for private guests, if you catch my meaning," Franks said with a laugh.

Jacobs thought it was kind of comical how he tried to play everything off. He did wonder how he seemed to know so much about the place, though. "So how do you know all this?"

"Uh, what?"

"You seem like you know quite a bit about it."

"Oh, well, you know, you hear things."

"Something tells me that you were on the receiving end of Lucy or Deb's work," Jacobs said.

"I cannot confirm nor deny those allegations," Franks said with another laugh, finding it amusing.

"All right. Thanks for the tip."

"Hey, remember where you didn't get it."

"Already forgotten."

As soon as Franks hung up, he went into the back office to clean up a few things. While he was back there, he heard the front door open and close. He quickly came back out, dismayed to see who was paying him a visit. It was Cedeno with four of his thugs by his side. It'd been a while since they'd seen each other and Franks wasn't particularly fond of having him in his store, especially after what happened with him and Jacobs. Franks immediately put on a happy face to pretend like they were old buddies.

"Hey, Ronnie. What's going on, man? It's been a while. What do I owe the pleasure of this visit?"

"You can skip the formalities, Eddie."

"OK. What can I help you with?"

"You can tell me who the clown was that robbed me of my merchandise, my money, and killed three of my men."

Franks shrugged. "I don't know, Ronnie. Why come to me?"

"Because the dude was seen coming in here."

"He was? Gee, news to me," Franks said.

Cedeno didn't look very happy at how the conversation was going so far. "Eddie, you know I don't like to play games. The guy said he was a cop. Now, maybe he is, maybe he's not. But you have a way of knowing everything about everyone."

Franks smiled, taking it as a compliment. "Just a talent I picked up over the years."

"The guy was seen coming in here. That means he did business with you. Now, maybe you're the one who told him where I was. Maybe you're the one who told him what I was doing. Maybe you're the one who put him up to it."

"Oh, come on, Ronnie, you know I'd never do that, man. I wouldn't jeopardize my reputation on someone looking to knock you over."

"Then what was he doing here?"

"Well, if it's the guy I'm thinking of, he came in here and said he had just quit the police," Franks said, trying to think of what else he could say to get himself off the hook. "He said he needed guns and heard your place was a front. He knew I had a record, so he thought I could help him."

"And did you?"

"Of course not, man. Look, I told him flat out, I said, don't mess with Cedeno, man. If you go over there and mess with him, he will take you out, he will kill you. That's exactly what I told him. I said, if you go over there, Cedeno will put you in a box."

"Looks like he didn't take your advice."

"I told him you'd come after him."

"What's this guy's name?" Cedeno asked.

"Uh, Jacobs, I think. Yeah, Brett Jacobs."

"So where can I find this Brett Jacobs?"

Getting nervous about what was going to happen to him, Franks started devising a plan in his head to fix the situation. "Uh, you know what? I think I actually have his phone number. Yeah, he left it in case I could help him. Obviously, I couldn't, but let me see."

Franks looked under the counter, pretending to move stuff around to find the number.

"Oh, here it is. I got it."

"Call him," Cedeno said forcefully.

"Call him?"

"Yes. Now."

"You mean right now?"

Cedeno pulled his gun out and pointed it at Franks. "Yes. I mean right now."

Franks felt sweat forming on his forehead. "Oh, yeah, no problem. I'll just get him on the phone right now. You want me to get him down here for you?"

Cedeno raised his eyebrows and nodded. He didn't need to say anything. Franks called Jacobs' number, getting the former cop after a couple of rings.

"Hey, man, this is Eddie Franks."

"Yeah, I know."

"Well, I guess you're wondering why I called since I told you the other day I couldn't help you."

"Huh?"

Franks was hoping that if he rambled on in what seemed to be an incoherent manner, that Jacobs would eventually pick up on the fact that something was wrong. Franks also hoped that he'd pick up on the clues that he'd start dropping.

"So, I was hoping you could come down here right now, I might have some information for you."

"About what?" Jacobs asked.

"About Cedeno, man, he's pissed about what you did to him. I hear he's looking for you right now. If you come in, I can tell you where to hide out and all."

"I don't need to hide out."

Jacobs didn't seem to be picking up the clues and Franks was starting to get a little nervous, thinking that if he didn't come down to his shop, that Cedeno might take him out first.

"What's that?" Franks asked to a phantom question. "No, you don't wanna go in that front door. They'll blast you for sure. Always look for another entrance, my friend."

"What are you talking about?"

"So, there's five? Yeah, OK. So that's good."

"Are you OK?"

"No, man, no way."

Jacobs finally understood that Franks was in trouble. Franks looked at Cedeno and shrugged.

Cedeno whispered, low enough that Jacobs wouldn't hear him, but loud enough for Franks to get the message. "Get him here now." Franks put his finger in the air and nodded, letting him know he would.

"Have you got company there right now?" Jacobs asked.

"What? Yeah, but listen, I can help you with that if you just come in now."

"There's five of them?"

"Sure, I'll take care of that."

"Go through the back?"

"Yeah, it'll be available," Franks answered. "Just come in the front door."

"Should I bring guns?"

"As many as you can get."

"When?"

"I dunno. Can you get here in ten minutes?"

"I'll be there in twenty," Jacobs said.

"All right. Yeah, I can wait thirty minutes," Franks said, putting his thumb up to placate Cedeno.

"Don't worry. I'll get you out of it."

Franks did feel a small sense of relief, though seeing a violent man like Cedeno in front of him helped to ratchet his fears up a notch. Once they hung up, Franks put his phone down on the counter and let Cedeno know Jacobs was coming.

"He's on his way, man."

"When?" Cedeno asked.

"Thirty minutes. He'll come right through the front door."

Though Cedeno wasn't exactly the most patient of people, thirty minutes wasn't so long to wait. He figured he'd pass the time by continuing to quiz Franks.

"So how do you suppose he knew where to hit me?"

Franks threw his hands up. "I dunno, man, he was a cop, he probably already had all that information."

"And you did not help him in any manner?"

"No way, man. I only met him the one time. Takes me a few meetings just to get comfortable enough around people to make sure I can help them. With him being a cop, it didn't feel right to me so I passed. You know I've been in jail before, I'm not looking to go back by getting mixed up with some cop. He said he was an ex-cop, but who knows if he was even on the level?"

Cedeno nodded, appearing to accept Franks' explanation, though he still threw down a heavy warning. "For your sake, you better not be lying to me."

"Ronnie, why would you even think that? Have we

ever not been on good terms before? Every time you've ever needed something, I've gotten it for you. Every time. We've never had any ill will."

Cedeno nodded again, agreeing with the statement. "I'll take you at your word this time, Eddie. But if I ever find out that you're lying to me, you know where you'll end up."

Franks shrugged, making it seem like it didn't bother him. "Ain't nothing to find out, man. I ain't worried. Me and you are cool. Always will be."

The conversation continued sporadically over the next twenty minutes. Sometimes it was between Cedeno and Franks. Sometimes it was Cedeno and his men. Cedeno's patience level was almost running out. He was getting anxious to get some payback on Jacobs for the stunts he pulled on him. He kept looking at the time. He thought he could wait out thirty minutes, but it seemed much longer than that.

Franks also was checking the time. He knew Jacobs would be there any minute. Franks just hoped he didn't come in cop-mode and try to talk down everyone to diffuse the situation. He hoped he'd come with guns blazing. Because he knew that Cedeno wasn't in the mood for talking. And if he wasn't taken out now, he'd always be a thorn in both of their sides.

11

JACOBS HAD BEEN at Eddie's shop for a few minutes. He parked in the alley in back of it, further down the street so he wouldn't be spotted in case Cedeno had a lookout. While there were some men who wouldn't have bothered to come, figuring it wasn't their problem, Jacobs felt differently. While Franks did have his hand mostly on the other side of the law, he didn't appear to be a bad guy, and he had helped Jacobs out several times already. He seemed like a guy he could trust. Plus, he could've just lured Jacobs down there into a trap and allowed Cedeno and his men to kill him. But he didn't do that. Franks warned him about the trouble. So, if Franks was in trouble because of the mess that Jacobs created, he had to go down and help him get out of it. There was nothing to think about or debate in his mind. It just had to be done.

Jacobs brought three handguns with him. One primary and two backups which he hid inside his jacket. He also had a couple of smoke bombs, courtesy of Cedeno. It was one of the things Jacobs found and stuffed into the bags he left with. Once at the back door of the pawn shop, he slowly opened it, not sure if he'd run into trouble immediately. Much to his surprise, as he went inside, he didn't. He crawled along the floor, just in case bullets started flying in his direction, figuring they wouldn't be aiming that low if they were expecting him.

While the others were waiting inside the main store, Cedeno was pacing around. He was obviously overanxious.

"Where is he? Where is he?" Cedeno asked.

"Relax, man, he's still got five minutes," Franks answered.

Cedeno stopped and looked toward the door behind the counter. He thought he heard a noise. "What was that?"

Franks heard it too and was reasonably sure what it was, but tried to play it off. "What was what?"

"That noise. I heard something coming from back there. Sounded like something scratching a door or a wall or something."

"Oh, that? Oh, that was probably just the cat."

"Cat?"

"Yeah, I have a little house cat back there. Helps to

keep the mice away. He roams around, knocks stuff over sometimes. Nothing to worry about."

Cedeno wasn't convinced, though. He nodded to one of his men to check it out. He then looked at Franks again. "If you're lying to me, you're a dead man."

Franks threw his hands up again. "How many times we gonna go through this?"

Cedeno, and the rest of his team, readied themselves in case of trouble, ready to fire their guns if need be. He then pointed at two of his men, then toward the front door. "You guys keep an eye out there."

Cedeno and his other man kept their attention diverted between the two doors.

"You want me to go back there and get the cat for you?" Franks asked, knowing full well that he wouldn't return with one.

"You stay put."

"All right, suit yourself." Franks turned to the man about to go in the back. "Just be careful. He has a tendency to scratch people he's not familiar with sometimes."

The man turned back toward Cedeno, who just motioned for him to go back there. The man did, and just as he went through the door, Cedeno started having second thoughts about the situation. He tapped one of his other men on the arm and told him to follow the guy into the back room.

Jacobs saw both men come through the door. He

was in a dark corner of the room, kneeling next to some large boxes stacked on top of each other. The two men were walking around the room, not really sure what they were about to find, if anything. Jacobs really didn't want to shoot the men, but it didn't look like he had any other options. He was hoping he could somehow knock them out or temporarily put them out of commission, but he didn't have any other tools to work with, other than his guns. And knowing there were three more men in the main part of the store, Jacobs knew he couldn't just stand there and slug it out with the two men. As soon as they started raising a ruckus, the others would probably run back there before he was able to do anything about it. While killing was what he intended to do with Mallette's men, he didn't really have a quarrel with these people, though he understood why they had one with him. But he also knew that, while he didn't really want to end their lives, if he didn't, it was likely he'd have to keep dealing with them over and over again. That was a prospect he wasn't fond of.

Jacobs reached into his pocket and put a silencer on the end of the barrel of his gun. It was also one of the things he found when he raided Cedeno's stash. He brought it in just in case, figuring something like this was a possibility. He didn't want the whole neighborhood to hear shots and converge on the store before he was able to get out. Jacobs waited a few seconds, wanting the men to get in the right position before unloading on them. Once they did, he let them have it. The first man was standing near the boxes and just as he turned around, Jacobs fired a round into his chest. As soon as he hit the ground, the other man started frantically looking around, wondering where the shot came from. He never saw Jacobs at all. The man began waving his gun around, just looking for a target to shoot at. He never got one. Jacobs fired another shot, also hitting the man in the chest. As the man slumped to the ground, Jacobs came out from behind the boxes and into the open.

Cedeno, along with everybody else, heard the noises, though they weren't sure it was gunfire. They also heard the bodies thumping hard onto the ground, but they weren't sure that's what it was. The door was still slightly open, though it had a tendency to close even when it wasn't what someone intended. The hinges on it needed tightening and it was something that Franks just never got around to doing. But it worked out better for this purpose as it prevented Cedeno from getting a clear look into the back room.

"What's going on back there?" Cedeno asked.

Worried that he wasn't getting a reply, concern grasped his face as he looked at Franks. Franks looked back at him and shook his head, pretending like he had no idea what was going on. Cedeno moved a little closer to the door, while looking back to the men guarding the entrance. Jacobs heard Cedeno's voice and could tell he wasn't too far away. Without knowing the exact positioning of everyone in the store, Jacobs wasn't in much of a hurry to get in there and engage in a gunfight. He'd rather move in a stealthier manner. He hurried over next to the door and clung to the wall.

Cedeno stopped moving toward the door and stood dead in his tracks, getting worried about what was on the other side of that door. "Is that you, Jacobs?"

There was no reply. Everyone was silent. Cedeno looked at both Franks and his other two men. After a few more seconds of worry, Cedeno waved for his remaining men to follow him into the back. None of them were eager to see what was back there, though. Believing he'd already lost two of his men, Cedeno wasn't itching to go back there either. He thought they could probably get the job done from where they were. If they just sprayed the wall and door with bullets, some of them would penetrate through to the other side, and hopefully a few would find their intended target. Before he had a chance to implement his plan, Jacobs sprang into action. He peeled himself from the wall and pulled the pin on his smoke grenade. He put his hand just beyond the edge of the door and threw it inside the main part of the store. Grey smoke immediately started filling up the store.

Knowing what was about to happen, Franks quickly hit the ground, hoping to stay out of the line of fire. As the others started coughing, Jacobs knew they weren't paying as close attention to the door as they should have been, and took that as his chance to rush through it. As soon as he did, Cedeno noticed a shadowy figure race into the room. He assumed it was Jacobs, and while one hand was covering his mouth as he was coughing, he raised his other hand that had the gun in it and fired a couple rounds toward the door. The shots missed, but Jacobs saw the muzzle flash from Cedeno's gun and instantly returned fire, unleashing a couple rounds of his own. Cedeno went down, one of the bullets going through his forehead.

Jacobs found himself behind the counter and noticed a body moving along the floor a few inches away from him. He was about to fire, but looked a little closer and saw the person pick their head up. It was Franks. He coughed and gave Jacobs a thumbs up sign.

"Nice to see you," Franks said, waving the smoke out of his face. "Kind of."

Jacobs knelt next to him to make sure he'd be able to hear him. "I think I got one up here. That makes three. Where's the other two?"

"They were near the front door."

Jacobs, while still staying low to the ground, went to the edge of the counter. He peered around it, looking to see if he could see the outlines of the remaining two members of the group. He struggled to see through the smoke, though it didn't seem to be quite as heavy in the front part of the store. Jacobs crawled along the floor, making sure he didn't make a noise to give himself away. After a minute, he saw the legs of one of the men. They were constantly moving about, mostly standing in the same area. It appeared that the man was looking around to see where he should be shooting, or where their attacker was. He couldn't find him. But it gave Jacobs a good idea where he should aim. Based on where the man's legs were, Jacobs raised his gun up slightly, taking aim at where he assumed the man's upper torso would be. He fired several rounds in quick succession. Within a few seconds, the man dropped to the floor. Jacobs could feel the vibration of the floor from the man's violent thumping on the ground.

Almost immediately after the man dropped, his partner by the door called out his name, concerned about what happened to him. It was a fatal mistake, as it allowed Jacobs to get a gauge on the man's position. Jacobs fired a few more shots at the direction of the voice. He heard the man grunt and groan. A couple more shots were heard, presumably from the other man shooting at where he hoped Jacobs would be. None of the shots seemed to come that close to him. Jacobs used the sound of the other man's gun as a guide to unload a few more rounds in his direction. He heard more moaning sounds as the man eventually hit the ground, joining his friends in death.

While hiding behind the counter, Franks was counting the number of bodies he heard hitting the floor. Assuming that everyone was dead, he raised his head above the counter.

"Is that it?"

Jacobs took a minute before responding, waiting to see if someone shot in Franks' direction after hearing him speak. He wasn't going to risk revealing himself and getting a bullet in return. But since nobody else was shooting, Jacobs assumed that everyone was dead. Without being able to see everyone right away, his main concern was that one or more of them might have been injured, but not dead. That would mean that they were still able to shoot and possibly kill him. But since there were no other shots heard, Jacobs thought it was a safe conclusion that they were all dead.

"Jacobs?" Franks asked, getting nervous as to whether he'd been killed as well.

Jacobs got back to his knees. "I'm here."

Franks felt a little better about the situation and moved around the counter and out into the open. "They all gone?"

"Seems that way."

The smoke started to dissipate, allowing Jacobs to move around the store and the bodies to become more visible. He went over to the two men near the door fist. He knelt beside them and checked their vital signs. Both were gone. He then saw Cedeno's body lying in the middle of the floor, his face clearly visible through an open patch of smoke. Jacobs saw the blood running down Cedeno's face from the bullet hole in the middle of his forehead. There was no doubt that he was dead. No checking was necessary. Jacobs then went back through the door to the office area to check his first two victims. Knowing there were more people waiting for him in the store, Jacobs never checked to make sure they were dead. He assumed they were since he didn't have to deal with them again after initially shooting them, but he'd rather make sure than take a stupid chance and wind up taking a bullet that he shouldn't have taken.

While Jacobs was checking the victims, Franks had opened a window to allow some of the smoke to get out of the store. After waving some of the smoke away from him, he just stood there with his hands on his hips, surveying the damage. He shook his head as he looked at all the dead bodies. A minute later, Jacobs came back in.

"You all right?" Jacobs asked.

"Yeah, no holes in me, man."

"Good. Well, I'm gonna take off before the police get here. They're probably already on their way."

"Wait. What?"

"I said I'm gonna leave before the police get here. I'm sure somebody heard the shots and called. They'll probably be here in a few minutes."

"And you're leaving?" Franks said, incredulous that he wasn't staying with him.

"Yeah, well, me and the police aren't exactly on great terms these days. I can't be here."

"You're their buddy. They ain't gonna lock you up."

"I already got word somebody spotted me from

my initial encounter with them at the dry-cleaning store," Jacobs said. "I don't think they're gonna think too much of me being here for this. And the number of friends I have on the force are dwindling by the day."

"So you're gonna let me take the rap for this?"

Jacobs shrugged. "You won't go down for this."

"Oh yeah? There's five dead bodies in my store, man. What do you think they're gonna assume?"

"Probably that you're mixed up with some shady people. Don't worry about it. They'll check your hands for residue, check your clothes for powder burns, you'll be fine."

"I'm glad you're so sure," Franks said.

"Trust me. They won't think you did it. Just don't tell them I was here."

"How am I gonna explain all this? The shooting, the dead bodies, the gang members on the floor of my store, the smoke bomb going off."

"Just tell them a bunch of these guys came into the store. Six, eight, ten, something like that, and they started turning on each other. They started shooting at each other, and the ones who were left ran out the back or something."

"I'm glad you got it all figured out," Franks replied.

Jacobs shrugged. "Hey, you called me. I didn't have to show up here. I could've just left you here to your own devices."

"Yeah, I guess that's true. But it wouldn't have

happened if you didn't go up there and take their place apart and kill them dudes."

"And I wouldn't have gone up there to begin with if you hadn't given me their names and told me that you didn't like them anyway," Jacobs said, having an answer for everything.

Franks sighed, knowing he was beat. "I hate it when people use what I do and say against me."

"Hey, if it comes to it, I'll come down and bail you out."

Jacobs smiled, though Franks didn't see much humor in it. "Thanks," he sarcastically replied.

"All right, if you need anything else, you know where I am."

"Unfortunately."

Jacobs then rushed out the back of the store. Once he was in the alley, he started hearing the police sirens and they were getting closer. He ran down to the end of the alley, hoping he could get out of there before the police were able to block off the area. When he reached his car, he quickly got in and raced out of the area. He got on the main road just as a few police cars zipped past him on the way to the pawn shop. Jacobs was happy that he was able to get away safely, and that Cedeno was no longer an issue, though he didn't feel particularly good about killing five people. He knew that it was necessary, as Cedeno would always be a thorn in his side, waiting just around the corner for him somewhere. He also was glad that Franks wasn't hurt in the fracas. And though the store owner would have some explaining to do for all that went down, Jacobs knew that he wouldn't take the fall for the incident. All things considered, it couldn't have gone much better for him.

12

THOUGH JACOBS WAS REASONABLY sure how everything would play out after the pawn shop incident, at least on the police side, he still felt a little badly for Franks that he got caught up in it. Just to make sure that he wasn't thrown for a loop, Jacobs checked in with him again after darkness set in.

"Hey, just wanted to make sure you weren't in the slammer yet," Jacobs joked.

"Ha ha. Man, you know the police and I don't mix well. I always get nervous when the boys in blue are around."

"Since we're having this conversation, I take it that they believed you weren't involved."

"Yeah, it pretty much went down like you said it would."

"What'd you tell them?"

"Pretty much what you told me to," Franks

answered. "Just said a bunch of them came in, a few of them got into some kind of argument, next thing I know, bullets are flying and I'm hiding underneath the counter."

"Good thing they didn't ask to see the video."

"What video?"

"The video you got."

"I don't have any video."

"The first time I went in there and talked to you, you said something about having the conversation on video."

Franks laughed. "Oh. That. Yeah, I kinda lied to you about that one. There ain't no video in here."

"You son of a...," Jacobs said, his voice trailing off before he finished.

Franks laughed again. "One of the things you should know about me, sometimes I make things up as I go along."

"I've noticed." Before moving on to a new topic, Jacobs thought back to the pawn shop, remembering that he saw what looked like cameras set up in the corners of the store. "Hey, I thought I saw a few cameras in there."

"Oh, well, yeah, there are cameras set up. But the system ain't working right now. I dunno, something with the wiring. I've been meaning to get it fixed one of these days, but I just haven't gotten around to it yet."

"How long's it been out?" Jacobs asked.

"Oh, about a year I guess."

Jacobs laughed to himself. "Oh. Well, as long as you're gonna get around to it one of these days."

"Keeps slipping my mind. Plus, I got other things to do that are more important, you know how it is."

"Yeah, that reminds me, speaking of things that are more important, I got a few questions for you."

"Oh, man, why do I get the feeling that this is gonna be more bad news for me?" Franks asked.

"What else can you tell me about the whereabouts of Mallette's crew?"

"Nothing, man."

"You sure about that?"

"Yeah. Listen, I told you before, I ain't exactly friends with those cats. Now that they seem to be in the wind, beats me where they wound up. From what I hear, they haven't gone back to any of their former stomping grounds."

"Yeah, I've already checked a couple places out."

"Check out that massage place I told you about. One of them girls might know something."

"I guess I'll just have to do that," Jacobs said. "What time is that place usually open until?"

"Around ten, I think. Unless you have a little after-hours party scheduled."

Jacobs went down to the address of the massage place that Franks had given him. It was almost closing time, but he figured he'd disrupt things less by getting there at almost ten, hoping most everyone had filtered out by that point. Almost immediately after going through the front door, he was greeted by a pretty, brown-haired receptionist.

"Can I help you?"

Jacobs felt a little uncomfortable just being there. "Uh, yeah, I'd, Uh, like a number five?"

The receptionist smiled, seeing the nervousness on his face. "Is this your first time being here?"

"Uh, yeah."

"It shows."

"Oh. Sorry."

"No need to apologize." She hit a button under the desk, unleashing a buzzing sound, to unlock the door to her right. "You can go in."

Jacobs went over to the door and opened it slowly, like he was afraid of seeing what was inside. "Umm, where do I go?"

The receptionist smiled again, thinking he was cute. "Just go down the hall, last door on your left."

Jacobs nodded. "Thank you."

"Enjoy yourself."

He walked down the hallway, passing a few other doors on both sides of him. It was a brightly lit place, pictures on the wall of various landscapes, not quite what he thought it was going to look like when he envisioned it. He pictured it being some dimly lit place where you could barely see a few feet in front of you. Once Jacobs got down to the end of the hallway, he turned the handle of the last door on his left. He peeked inside, unsure what he was going to see. It turned out he was all alone, at least for the moment. The room was pretty well furnished, with a couch, a small bed, and a chair. Jacobs sat down in the corner of the room in the chair, waiting for someone to enter.

It was a short wait. A pretty blonde came walking in about five minutes later. She was a little on the short side, standing no more than five-one or so, but she was well built in all the places that the men seemed to like. She was wearing nothing but a silky red robe that barely covered much, exposing parts of her breasts and most of her thighs. Another inch shorter and there would've been nothing left to the imagination.

"Hello," she pleasantly said, smiling.

"Hi."

"So, I'm Lucy. I don't think I've seen you before. Is this your first time?"

"Uh, yeah."

"Oh. Well, don't worry, I'll take care of everything. You just sit back and relax."

"I'm not here for that."

"You're not? Then what do you want?"

"I just wanna talk," Jacobs answered.

Lucy looked a little disappointed for several reasons. First, Jacobs was actually a good-looking guy. She didn't find most of the men who came in there that appealing. Second, every now and then she'd get someone who just wanted to talk. And usually she found them pretty creepy. "Fine," she said, tightening her robe.

Jacobs could see she wasn't really happy about it. "Is that OK?"

"Yeah, yeah. I get them like you every now and then. Men who just wanna come in here and talk."

"I'd think you'd be relieved with... not having to do other things."

"Yeah, well, most of the times when men just wanna talk, it winds up grossing me out. Some really weird people out there, you know."

"I'll try not to be one of those."

Lucy still didn't look very pleased, but went over to the couch and sat down. "You don't need to be rubbed or anything, do you?"

Jacobs looked perplexed. "Rubbed?"

"Yeah, some men want me stroking their hair, or just rubbing their leg as they talk. Really weird."

"Oh. No. You can just sit there."

"Oh, OK. Good. Listen, I'm still gonna have to charge you for this."

"Which is?"

"Hundred an hour," Lucy said.

Jacobs nodded, agreeing to her terms. "So how long you been doing this?"

Lucy shuffled in her seat. "Hey, this isn't gonna be one of those get-to-know-me sessions, is it? 'Cause I really don't like talking about myself much to people who come in here."

Jacobs leaned forward, figuring he should just come out and get what he was after out in the open quickly, instead of dancing around. "Listen, all I really wanna know is whether you know Lucky Frazier or any of the people he hangs out with."

Lucy looked up at the ceiling for a moment, pretending to be thinking. "No, don't think so."

"I've heard that you do."

"Look, what do you want from me?"

Jacobs tapped his leg with his middle finger, deciding how much he wanted to reveal to her. "Do you know Eddie Franks?"

A smile came over Lucy's face. "Sure, I know Eddie."

"You like him?"

"Yeah, Eddie's always good to me."

"Well, he sent me here."

"Why?"

"Because I'm looking for Lucky Frazier," Jacobs said.

"What for?"

"I have a present for him."

Lucy looked at him with distrust in her eyes, knowing that he had ulterior motives in mind. "What do you really want with him?"

"Before I tell you, I need to know whether you hang out with him? Friends, lovers?"

Lucy shook her head. "No, nothing like that. He's been in here a bunch of times, and he took me to dinner a few times, as well as a few other places, but I haven't seen him in a while."

"When was the last time?"

"About a month or so ago."

"Where?" Jacobs asked.

"In here. He said he had something big lined up and he wouldn't be around for a while."

Jacobs rubbed his eyes, knowing that must have been just before Frazier killed his family. "He didn't say where he was going?"

"Not to me."

"What about the other girl? Deb? Might she know something?"

"Not about Frazier. He always requested me. Why all the interest in him?"

"'Cause I plan on paying him a visit."

"You don't say that like you're friends."

"We're not," Jacobs said. "He took something from me and I intend to repay the favor with interest."

"What did he take?"

Jacobs looked at her with a ferocious intensity in his eyes. It actually scared her a little. "My family."

"Your family?"

"One month ago, he killed my wife and my children."

Lucy leaned back, horrified with what she was hearing, feeling bad for the man. She took her eyes off him and stared at the wall for a minute. "Hey, are you a cop?"

"Well, ex-cop now."

"I remember hearing about that. That was your family?"

Jacobs nodded. "Yep."

Though Lucy felt sorry for him, she also was thinking about her own predicament, with him being a cop. "Listen, you're not gonna take us in or anything, are you? I mean, we're not hurting anyone here."

Jacobs put his hand up to relieve her fears. "I'm not interested in turning you in. I quit the job a few days ago, anyway."

"Why? If you don't mind me asking?"

"Because I intend on making Frazier pay for what he did to me. Him and everyone else in Mallette's crew. Sooner or later I'm gonna find him."

Lucy fidgeted with her hands for a minute, debating with herself on whether she should tell all she knew. Part of her really felt for the man in front of her, as she could tell that he had a lot of pain in his heart. But she also didn't want to think of herself as a fink or something. Not that she especially liked Frazier. He was OK, but not really one of her favorites. Finally, she decided to help him out.

"Listen, I don't know if this will help you or not, but maybe it will."

"What?" Jacobs asked.

"He took me to an apartment a couple times. I don't even know if it was his or anything. But, maybe you could check there."

She remembered the address and told it to Jacobs,

who entered it into his phone. He was grateful for her help.

"Thank you."

"I'm sorry about what happened."

"Is there anything else you can think of?" Jacobs asked. "Other names he might have mentioned? Places? Anything like that?"

Lucy thought about it for a second, but nothing came to mind. "No. Sorry."

"Well, you gave me a place to start."

Jacobs got up and reached into his pocket, pulling out some cash. He walked over to Lucy and handed it to her. Since it looked like more than what she needed, she quickly counted it.

"This is two hundred," she said, looking confused.

"A small tip."

Because of the situation, she didn't even feel that good about taking the money at all. She wrinkled her nose and tried to hand the money back to him. "You know, you weren't even here that long. Don't worry about it. It was on me."

Jacobs took her hand and closed it, making a fist with the money still inside of it. He smiled at her. "A deal's a deal. Thank you."

Lucy smiled back at him, hoping she could do a little more for him. "You sure you wouldn't like to do something else while you're here? Still have a lot of time left."

"Maybe another time."

Lucy nodded, a little disappointed that they didn't get to roll around for a little bit. Jacobs walked to the door and then turned around. Hopeful that he changed his mind, she'd soon be disappointed again when he didn't.

"Do you think I could talk to the other girl? Deb?"

"What for?"

"Well, Eddie mentioned her name specifically," Jacobs answered. "If Frazier came to you, maybe she got some of his friends."

Lucy shrugged, not really having any idea. "Maybe."

"Could we check?"

Lucy slowly walked over to him and gave him another smile, touching his chin seductively with her hand. "Only for you."

They walked out of the room and went directly across the hall. Lucy started knocking on one of the other doors. "Deb, it's me."

A few seconds later, the door opened, a beautiful brunette stepping outside into the hall, closing the door behind her. She was completely naked and didn't seem to be embarrassed in the least.

"Sorry to bother you."

The well-endowed woman didn't seem to mind based on the pleasant look on her face. "Oh, no big deal. We just finished up anyway."

Though Jacobs couldn't help but take a few glances down at the large breasts that were staring him in the face, he tried to keep his focus on Deb's eyes, as hard a task as that was.

"So, what's up?" Deb asked. She looked Jacobs over and liked what she saw. She was hoping for a little more action between all of them. "A little threesome?"

"Don't I wish?" Lucy replied.

Deb put her hands on Jacobs' shirt and rubbed his chest. "So, what'd you have in mind?"

"Just a few questions."

Deb looked confused and then turned to her friend. "Huh? Is he putting me on?"

"Unfortunately not."

"What kind of questions? Dirty ones?"

"No," Jacobs said.

"And you disturbed me for this?" Deb asked, putting her hand up.

"Deb, just listen," Lucy said. "It's important."

Since Lucy didn't usually speak in that tone, Deb knew it must have been an important and serious topic.

"I'm looking for Lucky Frazier, any of his friends, or any of Rich Mallette's crew," Jacobs said. "You know any of them?"

Deb stared at him for a few seconds, then looked at Lucy for guidance. She wasn't sure what was going on, but people just didn't come in there looking for the likes of Mallette's bunch without either being cops or having a death wish.

"You a cop?"

"Ex-cop," Jacobs answered.

Deb once again looked at Lucy, who closed her eyes and nodded, indicating that it was OK to talk to him. "He's on the level, Deb. You can trust him."

Deb still wasn't so sure and sighed, not really liking the questions, but reluctantly agreed to help anyway. "What do you want to know?"

"Do you know any of them? Where they might be?" Jacobs asked.

She hesitated in answering, but eventually conceded. "Yeah. Yeah, I know a couple of them."

"You know where they are?"

"First, you tell me what you want them for."

"Because I'm going to take out every single person who works for Rich Mallette."

Deb was a little taken aback by his bluntness. She actually thought he sounded a little crazy. "Boy, you do have a death wish, don't you?"

"They killed my family. I'm gonna make them pay for that."

Deb looked at Lucy again to see if he was on the level. By Lucy's face, she could tell that he was. Upon hearing him talk about his family again, Lucy got a sad look on her face and looked down at the floor. She only ever did that when unpleasant news was being spoken of. Deb stared at Jacobs' face again, thinking that it looked familiar. Then it came to her.

"Wait a minute, you're that cop I read and heard about."

"Ex-cop," Jacobs repeated.

"I remember seeing your picture now."

"So, can you help me?"

"Well, I dunno, they're good clients."

"Deb!" Lucy said, giving her a stern look.

Deb rolled her eyes. Lucy was always the softer one of the two. She was always the one who could get swept up in a good sob story.

"This is about more than money or business," Lucy said.

"Oh, all right, all right," Deb replied.

"When did you last see any of them?"

"About two nights ago."

Jacobs was more than a little surprised by the revelation. He didn't think any of them would have shown their faces in the last few weeks.

"Who was it?" Jacobs asked.

"Guy's name was Gnat."

"Gnat Steckenridge?"

"Yeah."

"You know him?" Lucy asked.

Jacobs nodded. "I went undercover in Mallette's organization for a while. I've heard most of the names before. Haven't met him. Haven't met most of them, actually, but I know the name."

Lucy thought it was a strange name as the look on her face proved. "Why do they call him that? That can't really be his name."

"From what I understand, it's because he's always

hanging around, kind of like a gnat. Got to swat them away to get rid of them."

"Lucky, Gnat, do all these guys have nicknames?"

"Most of them. They think it makes them cool or something."

Jacobs turned his attention back to Deb and was about to pepper her with some more questions, when the door behind her opened up again. A fully clothed man stood in the doorway, looking a little alarmed at three people standing in front of him.

"Hiya," the man sheepishly said.

Jacobs nodded, not having any words for him. The man took that as a cue to take off and gave them all a wave and rushed down the hallway to leave.

"See you next week, John," Deb shouted.

"Regular?" Jacobs asked. Deb shrugged. "Anyway, you ever go anywhere with him?"

"No, I've only met him here. I don't meet anyone outside of here, unlike some people we know," she said, looking at Lucy. "Some people are more gullible than others."

Lucy rolled her eyes, hearing the criticism before. "I haven't done it in a while."

"He ever say anything to you while he's been here?" Jacobs asked. "Places he's gone, other people he knows, plans, anything like that?"

"He told me that he probably wouldn't be back for a few months," Deb said, trying to recall their conversation. "You know, not a lot of talking gets done in these things. They're not all like you, you know. Most just wanna get into the action."

"He say anything else?"

"I'm thinking, I'm thinking. He did mention some guy's name. I never heard it before so I didn't even bother asking what he meant."

"What was it?"

"Let me think and remember the context." After a minute of getting it straight in her mind, Deb remembered exactly. "Now I remember. He said he wouldn't be back for a few months. So I asked why. He said it was because he and the rest of the boys were leaving town next week."

"He say where they were going?" Jacobs asked.

"No, he didn't. But I asked why they were leaving so soon. And he replied that they'd have left even sooner if it wasn't for some guy not helping them."

"What was his name?"

Deb put her hand on her chin, trying to think. "It wasn't an American name. It was Asian I think. Sung maybe, or Sing..."

"Sang?"

"Yeah, that was it. Sang. They said the guy wouldn't help them so they had to use somebody else and it'd take a week to get everything together or something like that."

Lucy looked at Jacobs, who was processing the information. "That make sense to you?"

Jacobs looked back at her, and judging by the grin on his face, it did. "It's an extra piece to the puzzle."

"You know this Sang guy?"

Jacobs nodded. "I do."

"Maybe he'll be able to help you."

"He just might be able to at that."

"Anything else you need?" Deb said, putting her hand on the frame of the door to give him an even closer and better look at her body.

Jacobs raised his eyebrows, not used to such a forthcoming woman. He looked her over quickly, then glanced into the room. "Think you might need to clean up in there first."

Deb couldn't help but laugh. She shook her head, then went back into the room, closing the door.

"Well, thanks for the help," Jacobs said.

Lucy was kind of sad to see him go already and tried one last time to get him to stay. "Sure I couldn't interest you in a little nightcap?"

Jacobs was a little flattered that she took an interest in him, for whatever reason that may have been. But he couldn't ever see himself with another woman again, even a beautiful one, or a one-night stand. He wasn't ready for that so soon after Val passing and didn't think he ever would.

"Thanks for the offer, but I really should go."

Lucy nodded, knowing that would be his answer. Jacobs gave her a goodbye smile and walked past her. She turned and watched him get to the door to leave.

"Hey," she shouted. "You be careful."

"I will."

Jacobs put his hand on the door and was stopped once again.

"Hey. If you ever need anything again, feel free to stop by. Even if it's just to talk," she said with a smile.

13

Jacobs was waiting in Franks' pawn shop, waiting for Lee to arrive. After leaving the massage parlor, he called Franks to set up a meeting with the forger for the next day. They'd been waiting in the shop for about twenty minutes. Jacobs walked around, noticing the lack of blood on the floor.

"They did a nice job cleaning up."

"They were here almost all day, man," Franks said.

"Can hardly even tell anything happened here."

"Glad you think so. Things like this will keep people away for weeks. Word gets out, you know."

"Since when did you care if you actually got customers?" Jacobs asked.

Franks laughed. "Fair point. But I like to at least give the illusion that I got a nice, legit business going on."

"It's not much of an illusion."

"Ouch. What's with the sharp digs today? How'd you like Lucy and Deb last night, anyway?"

"Fine."

"I picture you as more of a Lucy type of guy."

"Is that so?"

"Yeah, she's more the sensitive type. Deb, she's more of the rip you apart type of girl. Good for certain occasions, you know what I mean?" Franks said, nudging Jacobs in the arm.

"I wouldn't know."

"They give you a special?"

"I didn't go there for fun," Jacobs answered. "I went there for information."

"All work and no play makes Brett a dull boy." Jacobs glared at him. Franks put his hands up. "All right, all right, I'm just saying, two beautiful women like that, gotta take advantage of your opportunities."

"We have different ideas of fun right now."

"So I see. What'd you want to see Sang about?"

"I was told Gnat Steckenridge had gone to see him recently about getting out of town with new information."

"Oh, man, I can't stand that guy. He's like such a little nuisance, you know?"

"So I've heard. Dealt with him much?"

"Nah, just a couple of times," Franks said. "Haven't seen him in a while. Must be about six months or so now."

The buzzer to the back door went off.

"Sang must be here."

"Doesn't he go through front doors?" Jacobs asked.

"Nah. He doesn't like the possibility of being spotted."

They went to the back, and upon seeing who it was, let him in. They all greeted each other, then went to the office to talk. Once they sat down, they got right to it.

"So, you said I didn't need to bring anything with me, so I take it this is some kind of information session," Lee said. "What's this about?"

Jacobs spoke right up. "I learned that a man came to you recently about getting some documents and you refused."

"That is nothing new. I'm besieged with requests all the time. I don't always accept."

"I know, but this time, the person who asked was Gnat Steckenridge."

Lee's face indicated he knew exactly who Jacobs was referring to. "Ah, yes, Mr. Steckenridge. So, what would you like to know?"

"Did he come to you?"

"Yes. Oh, must have been five, six days ago."

"You know he's one of Mallette's Maulers?" Jacobs asked.

"Yes."

"Well, you knew I was looking for them, why didn't you tell me that you were doing business with them?"

Lee put his finger up to correct him. "But I did not

do business with them. As a matter of fact, I did not even see him. It was a request through a third party."

Jacobs immediately looked over to Franks.

"Hey, don't look at me, man, I didn't handle that one," Franks said. "I'm not the only guy in town who does this stuff."

Lee smiled. "No, Eddie was not involved in this one. I use several people in my line of work. I don't like to rely on any one individual."

"You still could've let me know," Jacobs said.

"Mr. Jacobs, I sympathize with your quest for your own brand of justice, and I wish you luck in the same pursuit. But I work in forgery, creating identities, I am not an informant. I cannot just go running around, telling everyone my business and who contacts me. That would be bad for my business."

"So, you can't tell me anything about it?"

"I did not say that. I said I cannot run around and willfully divulge information to people like I'm some kind of street informant. But if someone asks me the right questions, I'm certainly not against answering them."

Jacobs smiled. "So Steckenridge came to you but you turned him down. Why?"

"It's actually a very simple reason. As I've told you before, I do not care for Mallette's men," Lee answered. "Unless I'm in dire need of money, I no longer work for any Tom, Dick, or Harry that comes to me for help. Since I've put myself in a good financial position over the last few years, I only work when I want to. When I feel the need. Or when someone comes to me with a story that I can't resist. Such as yours. So you see, I merely chose not to help him because I do not care for him."

"Was he mad?"

"I have no idea. I simply said that I was too busy to take on any new clients at the moment."

"Well, I was told that he was going to use someone else, but it probably wouldn't be for a few more days. Do you know who he might go to?"

Lee moved his head, thinking. After a minute, he nodded, believing he'd come up with the answer. "I believe I do. It's a short list. Probably only one or two people."

Lee reached onto the desk and tore off a piece of paper from a scratch pad and wrote down a couple names on it. He then passed it over to Jacobs. Jacobs read the names to himself, none of whom were familiar to him.

"You sure it'd be one of these two?" Jacobs asked.

"Almost positive. After me, they are the two best in the city. Mallette's boys are hot. They know it. If they want to disappear for a while, they'd have to use one of them. No question in my mind."

Though Jacobs felt a slight sense of relief in knowing who he was looking for, now, the question was how would he find them. "So how do I get in touch with these guys?"

Lee pulled his hands up, indicating he had no idea. "That is not my department. I have no need for their services so they are not in my phone book."

"But you know of them?"

"By reputation only. I've never met them."

Franks leaned forward in his seat and snapped his fingers at Jacobs to get his attention. Once Jacobs looked at him, Franks was motioning with his fingers to pass him the paper. Jacobs did, and Franks immediately looked over the names.

"Do you forget who you're talking to here?" Franks said. "I know everyone in this city. And if I don't, I know someone who does."

"So do you know them?" Jacobs asked.

"Sure do."

"You do?"

Franks rolled his eyes, pretending to be offended. "Yes, I do. Of course, man, what'd I just get done telling you? I know everyone."

Feeling like his part of the meeting was finished, Lee got up to leave. Before going, Jacobs wanted to make sure he had no other bits of information for him.

"One last thing," Jacobs said. "I feel like I should ask this since you don't volunteer information and only reveal something if asked."

"Go ahead."

"Have you had any other contact with Mallette's group lately?"

"No."

"Do you have any idea where they are or might be?"

"No," Lee said with a smile. "Good luck to you in your search."

After Lee left and Franks locked the back door, he went back to the office and sat across from Jacobs. Franks could tell he was deep in thought as he didn't seem to be paying him much attention.

"So what are you thinking?" Franks asked.

"I'm thinking I need to pay these guys a visit."

"How do you plan on doing that?"

Jacobs just looked at him, indicating he was going to be a big part of it. "Aww, man, not me again."

"You said it yourself, you know them."

"Yeah, but that doesn't mean I wanna get involved in anything again."

"You don't have to get involved," Jacobs said. "Just bring them here and I'll do the rest."

Franks almost fell out of his seat after hearing that. "Bring them here? And you're saying I don't have to get involved?"

"You don't."

Franks looked flustered and almost didn't know what to say. "How is bringing them here not getting involved?"

"I'll do all the talking."

"You're gonna wind up getting me killed, you know that?"

Jacobs thought he was over-exaggerating a little.

"Really? These guys aren't violent killers. They're basically pencil pushers."

"Says you. Why can't I just set something up for you somewhere and you go meet them there and do whatever it is you plan to do?"

"Won't that kind of undermine you a little?" Jacobs asked. "You might lose a bit of your reputation and future business."

"Let me worry about that."

"It'll be better this way."

"How you figure? It all amounts to the same thing."

"Not really."

"Well, I'd sure like to see how you figure that," Franks said.

"Well, if you stop getting so huffy and calm down, then I'll tell you."

Franks put his hands on his hips as he awaited the explanation. "I'm not huffy. Just... perplexed."

"Are these other two guys friends of yours?"

"Hardly."

"Frequent business partners?" Jacobs asked.

"Not really."

"No ties to them?"

"I only facilitate deals to them on the occasion that Sang's got other things to do. Or if he doesn't feel like doing it."

"So how often is that?"

"Few times a year, maybe."

"OK. So here's what I'm thinking."

Franks switched positions and folded his arms in front of his chest. "Can't wait to hear it."

"You have them come here."

"Not liking it so far."

Jacobs glanced up at him and stopped talking. "You gonna let me finish?"

Franks sat back down, figuring he'd take it better sitting. "I guess."

"You set up a meeting and have them come here. I'll tie you up in a chair..."

Franks shot up out of his chair, irritated. "Tie me up in a chair?! What are you, crazy or something? Why am I getting tied up in a chair? Tie yourself up in a chair."

Jacobs let Franks continue spouting off for another minute, patiently waiting for his blood to stop boiling. Jacobs didn't even bother looking at him for the most part, letting his eyes drift over to the wall as he finished his spiel.

"You done?" Jacobs asked.

Franks finally stopped puffing and looked at his visitor, ready to get a few more things off his chest. Before saying anything else, he suddenly stopped and sat down again.

"Now I'm done."

"You haven't even let me finish."

"Because I don't like it," Franks said.

"Why don't you let me finish before saying that you don't like it?"

"All right, man, all right, go ahead."

"Are you going to let me finish this time before interrupting me?"

"Yeah, yeah, go ahead."

"You set up a meeting with these guys here," Jacobs said. "Before they get here, I'll tie you up. Not hard or anything. That way it makes it seem like I forced the issue and made you call them. You can even say I threatened you. When I get the information I want, I let them go, I untie you, you get to still keep your reputation and have your contacts intact."

Franks stared at him for a good minute, thinking about it. It made sense, not that he wanted to admit it. "Why do I even have to get involved at all? This ain't my crusade, man."

"Well, do you want me in your face every couple of days while I look for these guys? This way, I get what I need faster, which means I'll get out of your hair faster."

"I like that part. Because you're becoming more of a pain than you're worth, you know that?"

Jacobs actually seemed to take some delight in the comment. He really didn't care what anyone thought of him at that point, as long as he got what he wanted. Jacobs sat there, waiting for Franks to confirm that he was willing to submit to his plan. Franks was purposely avoiding looking at Jacobs' face as he made a decision, not wanting to get railroaded somehow. When he finally did look at it, he could tell by Jacobs' face that he was looking for him to speed up the process. Franks sighed before answering, not liking what he was about to say.

"Yeah, man, sure, whatever. Just make sure I don't wind up with a couple bullets in me."

"Well, you said they weren't the violent type," Jacobs said.

"Everyone has their limits."

"Especially me."

14

IT WAS LATER that same night that Jacobs was back in Eddie's shop. Franks had called for a meeting with both Dick Mills and Stewart Williams, the consensus number two and three men in the business behind Lee. Jacobs requested that Franks set it up for different times for the two men to arrive, that way he had sufficient time to get the information he needed. Mills was scheduled for seven, Williams for ten.

Jacobs looked at the time and saw it was a few minutes before seven and they had to get in position. In the office in the back room, Franks hopped in the chair and Jacobs tied some ropes around him. It wasn't very tight, though, and if Franks was really trying, he would have been able to break free of them.

"Wait a minute," Franks said.

"What?"

"This isn't some elaborate plan to tie me up and take advantage of me or something, is it?"

Jacobs just shook his head. He had no words for him. Franks then started laughing.

"Hey, man, just joking. Trying to lighten the levity of the room."

Jacobs looked at him strangely, thinking that made no sense whatsoever. "Lighten the levity... I'm not even gonna try."

"You know, raise everyone's spirits."

"There's only you and me here."

"Yeah, and it feels cold in here."

"I'm lightened enough right now," Jacobs said.

"I feel it's best to try and bring some humor to everything I do."

"Is that so?"

"Yeah, I think your day goes by better and faster when you're in an upbeat mood," Franks replied. "It's some long hours working if you don't enjoy what you're doing. I mean, who wants to spend the entire day moping around?" He then glanced at Jacobs, who had a stern look on his face, and thought about his situation. "Well, maybe moping around is better in your case."

Jacobs looked at the time, hoping their visitor would come soon, just so he didn't have to listen to any more of Franks' nonsense.

"Hey, you are gonna let me out of this when you're done, right?"

"I'm still thinking about it."

"Seriously?"

Jacobs rolled his eyes, not believing he actually had to explain it. "They're not even tight. Did you even try wiggling loose?"

"Oh. No." Franks moved his hands and arms around, seeing that he actually had quite a bit of room.

"Hey, not too much. I don't wanna have to redo it again."

"Are you sure you gave yourself enough time? I mean, three hours between appointments is not that long."

"It's long enough," Jacobs said. "I only need a few minutes with each of them to get what I want."

"And what if neither one says anything? What then?"

"They'll talk."

"Why are you so sure?"

"'Cause they're not in the violent game. They don't want to be tortured."

"You're gonna torture them?"

"The thought of being tortured is sometimes worse than actually doing so."

"You say that like you have a lot of experience in the matter."

Jacobs gave a wry smile, thinking it was best to leave him guessing.

"Well, how 'bout this?" Franks said. "What if the first one says it's not him, and you believe him, and you let him go, then the second one says it wasn't him, and you believe him, then you think it was really the first guy all along? Huh? What then? Because then, you have to let the second guy go, and then you have nobody."

"Do you always talk this much?"

"Mostly. Especially when I'm in dire situations."

"This isn't a dire situation."

"Says the man who isn't tied up."

Jacobs eagerly watched the time tick by, hoping Mills would get there soon. Mostly so he wouldn't have to keep listening to Franks' endless jabber than anticipating the man's arrival.

"Which way's he gonna come in?" Jacobs asked.

"Oh, he'll buzz in from the back here."

"Does anybody come in the front?"

"Not really."

"Why don't you just build a secret compartment or entrance?"

Franks' face lit up, thinking about it. "You know, I've thought about that quite a bit over the years."

"Somehow that doesn't surprise me."

"Yeah, but you know, I think it's too much work."

"Is that right?"

"Yeah, I mean, that's a lot of construction work, don't you think?" Franks asked.

"Maybe."

"Plus, it'd be hard keeping that thing a secret."

"Especially with your mouth," Jacobs said.

"No, I mean with the actual construction. Everybody will be in here asking what's going on and all. How do you keep people from finding out about a thing like that?"

"How about you just close the store while it's happening? Or, maybe don't do any business here while it's going on?"

Franks nodded, liking the suggestion. "You know, that's a good point. A real good point."

"Glad you think so."

"I'm gonna keep that in mind."

"Good."

It was five minutes after seven and Jacobs was starting to worry that Mills wasn't going to show.

"You sure you said seven?"

"Relax man, he'll be here," Franks answered. "Not everyone is right on time and punctual, you know. Sometimes things get in the way. Life, women, traffic."

It was only a minute later that the back door started buzzing.

"See? There he is now," Franks said. "Right on cue."

Jacobs quickly shuffled to the door and looked out the peephole. Though he didn't know Mills on sight, he looked almost exactly the way that Franks had described him. Short, stocky, beard, and receding black hair that was tied back in a ponytail. He wore a light blue colored suit and had a briefcase in his hand. Jacobs opened the door, stepping to the side so Mills wouldn't see him at first. Mills came walking right in, not the slightest bit suspicious that he didn't see Franks at first.

Mills started talking before he was fully in the room or saw anyone. "So, what was this business you said you had for me?"

Jacobs closed the door behind him, slamming it shut. Mills jumped and turned around, seeing Jacobs standing there, staring at him with a menacing face.

"Who are you?" Mills asked.

Jacobs didn't answer. Instead, he just pointed to where he wanted Mills to go. Though Mills wasn't sure what was going on, he figured it was best to comply with the man's wishes. He walked over to where he was directed with Jacobs following closely behind him. He stopped and turned around, Jacobs just pointing again, this time, clear that he was pointing to the office. Mills walked into the office and immediately saw Franks tied up in a chair. He was growing increasingly worried about his own safety. Franks didn't wait for Mills to say anything, speaking up right away.

"Dick, man, sorry about all this, looks like you walked right into one, buddy."

"What's going on?"

"Looks like our friend here is looking for something."

"Looking for what?"

"I dunno. Something about something about something, I can't make heads or tails out of it. He made me call you, said he'd kill me if I didn't. Sorry, man, I didn't want to bring you into this, but he forced me to."

Mills took turns looking at Franks and the strange man next to them. Jacobs looked mean enough to kill both of them in an instant, Mills thought. As he waited to be told of the reason for him being there, he couldn't think of why he would be.

"Sit down," Jacobs sternly said, keeping up his tough appearance.

Mills did as he said, slowly sitting in the chair next to Franks. To keep the tough appearance up, Jacobs pulled out a gun so Mills could see that he had one. He pulled the magazine out and then quickly jammed it back in. Mills' eyes were fixated on the weapon as Jacobs toyed around with it.

"I want answers and I want the truth. And if I don't think I'm getting them, I can guarantee you that you're gonna wind up in a worse position than he is," Jacobs said, pointing to Franks.

"What do you want to know?" Mills sheepishly asked.

"Lucky Frazier, Gnat Steckenridge, or any other of Mallette's Maulers."

Mills looked over at Franks, not sure if this was for real. He licked his lips before answering, knowing that the man meant business.

"I... I don't understand what you want with me. What makes you think I can tell you?"

"They're looking to get out of town in the next few

days. I was told they contacted someone about forging some documents for them to help in that regard. That leads me to you."

Mills quickly looked at Franks, then back at Jacobs and shook his head. "Well, it wasn't me. I can assure you that."

"I don't believe it."

"No, it's the truth. It's not me."

Jacobs let out a deep sigh, letting Mills know that he wasn't happy. He paced around the room for a few seconds, slapping his thigh with his gun to make Mills think he might be using it soon. Sensing that his time left on the planet might have been dwindling with each passing second, Mills kept harping on the fact that he didn't help the pair that the stranger was looking for. He somehow had to make him believe it.

"Honest, I wouldn't lie to you," Mills said. "Not now. There's other guys besides me that do this sort of thing."

"I know that."

"Try Sang Lee. He's probably the best in the city."

"I already know Sang. It wasn't him," Jacobs said.

"Oh. Then try Stew Williams. If it wasn't me or Sang, it's probably him that you're looking for."

"I think you're just throwing names out to get yourself off the hook."

"I swear I'm not."

Hoping to somehow convince the man, Mills put

his briefcase on the desk, encouraging Jacobs to rifle through it if he was so inclined.

"Look through anything you want," Mills said.

He opened the briefcase and spun it around in Jacobs' direction. There was even a small laptop buried under some of the papers. Jacobs walked over to it and moved some of the paperwork around. Desperate to get himself out of the situation, Mills was willing to do just about anything to clear himself.

"I'll even log onto the computer for you," Mills said. "You can check my emails, downloads, documents, whatever you need."

By the lengths at which Mills was going to prove his innocence, Jacobs was confident that he wasn't the man he was looking for. He would have been much more guarded with his information if he was. Jacobs looked through a few of the papers in the briefcase just to be sure, but he didn't believe Mills was the guy. As Jacobs looked through the briefcase, Mills looked very tense sitting there, waiting silently as he hoped to be cleared. Once he was done, Jacobs made sure everything was back in the briefcase and closed it, spinning it around so the front lined up with Mills' seat.

"You can go," Jacobs said.

Though Mills was happy to hear the words, he looked a little surprised. He didn't expect to be let loose so soon, if at all. He did a double-take, looking at Jacobs, then at Franks.

"I... I can leave?" Mills asked, not wanting to make a wrong move.

"Out the back."

Mills eagerly picked up his briefcase and headed toward the door.

"Hope to see you again sometime, Eddie."

"Likewise, dude," Franks replied.

"Hey," Jacobs said, stopping Mills before he made it to the back door. Mills immediately turned around, hoping he wasn't about to play some sick, cruel joke on him, like he couldn't leave or shoot him. "You better have been telling me the truth."

"I give you my word."

"Because I'm gonna be talking to Williams soon. And if I find out that it really was you, you'll be seeing me again."

"I promise you that everything I said was the truth."

"It better be. 'Cause once you walk out that door, you're going to be followed by a friend of mine. I already know where you live, so you don't need to try and shake him. He was an expert tracker in the military, so don't try to go anywhere either, or else he'll cut your throat."

Mills started looking nervous again. "Understood."

"Just go home and if everything checks out, you'll be in the clear."

"How will I know?"

"Well, if you don't hear from me again tonight, then you'll know."

Mills anxiously nodded several times and hurried out the door. Once he left, Jacobs locked it as he waited for his next guest. He then went back to the office.

"Hey, you mind untying me for a little bit since we got some time to kill," Franks said. He then laughed as he thought about what he said. "Get it? Time to kill. Kind of a play on words there considering everything going on."

Jacobs rolled his eyes. "I'll untie you if you promise not to make any more stupid jokes the rest of the night."

"Done deal."

After Jacobs untied him and he was free from the restraints, Franks stood up, still having some questions about what was going on.

"I heard what you told Mills before he left. You really got some military tracker out there following him?"

"No."

"Oh. Well then, why'd you tell him that you did?"

"Wanted to keep him nervous," Jacobs said.

"You're sure he was leveling with you about not knowing them boys?"

"Yeah. I don't think he'd be that anxious and cooperative if he didn't. I mean, if you don't know them, then why let someone ruffle through your stuff and possibly find out that you did."

"'Cause maybe he does, and he knows there's nothing there that links him to them. Ever think of that?" Franks asked.

"Yeah. That's why I told him someone was following him."

"So, what are you gonna do if you're wrong? You don't actually have someone following him and you don't know where he lives. What are you gonna do then?"

"Have you set up another meeting with him?" Jacobs asked in a joking manner.

"Oh, real funny. Now who's making stupid jokes?"

"Figured I'd join the crowd."

"No, seriously, you ever think about what you're gonna do if this next guy tells you the same thing? What are you gonna do then?"

"He won't."

"How can you be so sure? What if they used someone other than these three guys?"

"They didn't."

"Why are you so sure of that?" Franks asked.

"Well, let me ask you a question."

"Shoot."

"If you're in hiding and want to get out of the hot zone, knowing the police or other people are after you, who would you go to?"

Franks moved his head around, understanding the point Jacobs was making. "I'd choose one of the best guys."

"Right, you don't go to an unknown or someone not as talented or good."

"Unless the big dogs all shoot you down."

"We all know money talks. If they shoot you down, you just keep upping the ante. Eventually someone would make room on their schedule."

"Yeah, I guess you're right there."

"Besides, according to Mills, he said he didn't even talk to them. That means they asked Sang first, then probably went to Williams, who accepted. So Mills was probably their third choice, which they didn't even get to."

"That's some smart police work right there," Franks said. "Ever think about being a cop someday?"

Franks laughed, but stopped upon seeing the glare he was receiving from Jacobs. "Didn't we make a deal about the jokes?"

"Oh, yeah, sorry. Just can't help myself sometimes."

Since they still had a little time to pass until Williams showed up, Jacobs and Franks sat down and talked for a while. Not really one of Jacobs' favorite activities, but it was probably better than just staring at the wall for two hours. Franks took it as an opportunity to get to know his new friend a little better.

"So, what are you gonna do when you find these guys?"

"You already know the answer to that," Jacobs replied.

"Yeah, I know about that, but what if you get the top dogs first? You still gonna go after the rest?"

"I want Rich Mallette's organization to crumble while he's in prison. I want no trace of it left. That means they all have to pay the price."

"All right, all right, I feel you on that. But he's got a lot of men. I don't think this is necessarily a battle you're gonna win in a few weeks or whatever."

"I've got time. I'm in it for the long haul."

"And when they're all gone? What are you gonna do then?"

Jacobs looked away and shook his head, honestly having no idea. "I don't know. Haven't thought that far ahead yet. Doesn't really matter, though."

"Why's that?"

"Because it's never gonna be truly over until Rich Mallette pays the price."

"But he's in prison, man," Franks said. "You gonna disguise yourself as a guard and take him out?"

"No, I'll wait until he's released."

"Isn't that gonna be like five or ten years? Something like that?"

"He didn't pull the trigger, but the order came from him. It started with him. It's gonna end with him."

15

_____

By the time ten o'clock rolled around, Jacobs and Franks were in their respective positions, just as they were for Mills. Franks was tied up in a chair in the office, Jacobs waiting by the back door. They planned on working it the same exact way.

"I'll be glad when this is over, man," Franks said, shouting to make sure he was heard.

"Just be quiet."

"You know this is kind of humiliating to a man who's got such a prestigious reputation as me. I mean, being tied up in a chair. I mean, really?"

"Don't you ever get tired of talking?"

"Not really."

"I noticed."

After a few more minutes, Jacobs was finally successful in getting Franks to quiet down. It was five minutes after ten when the back door started buzzing.

Jacobs looked through the peephole and saw Williams standing there. He was an older gentleman, probably in his late fifties, early sixties, with graying hair. He wore glasses and a suit.

After being let in, Jacobs surprised him, just as he did with Mills. He directed Williams to the office, who also had a briefcase in hand, and told him to sit down next to Franks.

"Hey, man, sorry about all this," Franks said. "I didn't have much choice either."

"What's going on?" Williams asked.

"What's with all the suits and briefcases with you guys?" Jacobs asked. "Is that like a professional thing with all of you?"

"Excuse me?"

"Never mind."

Williams stood up. "What is all this about? I demand to know what's going on here."

Jacobs was perturbed by his behavior and started fuming himself. "Sit down. I'll tell you what's going on when I'm ready."

Seeing that the man had a temper, Williams complied with his wishes and sat back down. He shuffled around in his seat as he waited for an explanation.

"I want to know about Lucky Frazier and Gnat Steckenridge," Jacobs said. "You know, Mallette's boys."

Williams' face didn't indicate any knowledge of them. "Who?"

"You gonna play that game with me? Do I really

look like the kind of guy who wants to play games here?"

"I really don't know what kind of guy you are."

Jacobs put his hand on the briefcase that was on the table and angrily slid it off, flinging it against the wall. "The kind that you don't mess with."

Williams stared at Jacobs, almost afraid to take his eyes off the man. "What do you want?"

"I already told you."

"Who are you?"

"It doesn't matter. All that matters is that you tell me what I want to know."

"I can't tell you what I don't know," Williams said. "I don't know any of them."

"Bullshit. You know them. They came to you a few days ago."

Williams shuffled around in his seat some more, trying to think of how he could get out of the situation. He was a little alarmed at how the man seemed to know his business. "There are other people besides me they could've gone to."

"Sang Lee and Dick Mills," Jacobs said, knowing he was gonna try that trick. "I've already checked them out. It's not them. That leaves you."

"There's hardly just the three of us that do business in this city."

"You're the main three. Men with as high a profile as Mallette's bunch, they wouldn't go to anybody else. They'd use the best."

Williams made a face, almost looking satisfied at being paid a compliment. "Well, that's true."

After a few more minutes of questioning, Williams kept deflecting having known any of the names he was asked about. But it was obvious to Jacobs that he was lying. Unlike Mills, Williams wasn't as forceful in how he answered anything. There was no question that he was holding back information.

Franks thought he would try to help things out from his end. "Man, if you know something, it's better to just come out and say it. Trust me, I've been tied up in this chair for like five hours now. It ain't gonna get better unless you just come clean."

Williams looked at him and cleared his throat, still feeling uneasy about everything. "After this is over, you can be sure I'll never answer any of your calls again."

Tired of the runaround, Jacobs slammed his fists down on the table, alarming the two men sitting down, causing both of them to jump in their seats. He glared at Williams as he spoke. "You won't have to worry about that, 'cause after this is over, you won't be able to call anyone again."

"I don't know how many times I can tell you that I don't know them."

"I don't know how many times I can tell you that I don't believe you."

Instead of continuing to go around and around for an extended amount of time, Jacobs figured he'd try another tactic to cut the interview short. He pulled out his gun and did the same trick he did with Mills. He pulled the magazine out and jammed it back in, letting Williams know it was loaded. Williams licked his dry lips, his eyes bulging out as he stared at the weapon.

"What are you gonna do with that?"

"Well, that depends on you," Jacobs answered.

"What's that supposed to mean?"

"You know, I used to be in the military."

"So?"

"So that means I'm trained in how to shoot someone in thirty different spots until they bleed out. That's an awful lot of pain a man can endure."

"So why are you telling me?"

"I dunno. How long you think you would last?" Jacobs asked.

Williams nervously looked over to Franks, hopeful that the man with the gun wouldn't do as he was boasting. Franks puffed, giving him a look that suggested not to call his bluff.

"I dunno, man, it's your life, but I'd think real hard about giving the wrong answer," Franks said.

Williams kept up with his nervous face, continuing to look between the two men, unsure how he should proceed. By not coming right out and maintaining his innocence on the subject, he was basically letting Jacobs know he was on the right path. It was easy to see the anguish on Williams' face as he contemplated what to do. He had been holding back, that much was clear to everyone.

"You know what you're gonna do to me?" Williams asked.

"I'm not gonna do anything to you as long as you give me the right answers. You tell me what I want to know, you get to walk out the way you came in. Still breathing."

"You're not gonna do anything to me?"

"I don't give a crap about you. All I want is Mallette's men."

"You're gonna ruin me. My reputation will be shot after this."

"No, it won't. 'Cause nobody will be alive to talk about it," Jacobs said. "They'll be dead. You'll be able to keep on doing what you do. That'll be the end of it."

"And what if they happen to kill you instead?"

"I guess that would be unfortunate."

"Unfortunate? For you maybe, but I'd be as good as dead. My reputation would be ruined, and that's just supposing that they'd let me live after that," Williams said.

"Well, as I see it, you got two choices right now. You can tell me what I want to know and hope that I make it through it in one piece."

"Or?"

"Or, I can just kill you right now so you don't have to worry about what happens later."

A lump went down Williams' throat. It wasn't much of a choice. And the man in front of him seemed crazy enough to shoot him right there. He would just have to hope that Mallette's men would never come back to him. Knowing he had no other options, he had to divulge what he knew.

Williams took a deep sigh before letting the cat out of the bag. "Fine. You win."

Jacobs took a quick look at Franks and nodded, but didn't maintain the glance long enough for Williams to figure out they were in cahoots. "So, what's the deal?"

"Steckenridge contacted me a few days ago about helping them with new identities."

"Were they going somewhere?"

"I'm not sure. I think he said something about St. Louis."

"When were you planning on meeting them?"

"Either tomorrow or the day after," Williams said.

"I think your plans are going to change there."

"Why?"

"Well now, unless you plan on dying today, I can't exactly let you leave here and risk you telling them. Can I?"

"I promise you I won't spill a word."

"Well, obviously you're a trustworthy individual," Jacobs sarcastically said. "But I'm sure you can see the logistical problem with that."

"So you're just gonna keep me here for a couple days?" Williams asked, his voice raised at the possibility.

"No, that wasn't quite what I had in mind."

"Then what?"

"You're gonna call them now and arrange a meeting tonight," Jacobs said.

"Tonight? How am I supposed to pull that off?"

"You're gonna tell them you've been working non-stop on it and finished early. Then you're gonna tell them that you have to give it to them tonight because you're going out of town for an emergency tomorrow."

"And what if they don't agree?"

"They'll agree. If they don't, then they're not getting what they need. They'll agree."

Sweat was starting to roll down Williams' face as he thought about the prospective meeting he'd be having later.

"So where were you supposed to have this little exchange of yours?" Jacobs asked.

Williams shrugged. "Nothing was set in stone."

"How 'bout the park?"

"No, they'll never go for that. It's too much in the open."

"Fine. Location doesn't matter anyway. Let them pick it."

"What time am I supposed to suggest?"

"Make it two hours from now."

Williams sighed, hating the predicament he was now in, though he realized he had no other choice but to cooperate.

"Make the call," Jacobs said.

"My phone's in my briefcase."

Jacobs walked around the desk and picked the

briefcase off the floor. He opened it and found the phone, tossing it to Williams. As he started hitting the buttons, Jacobs wanted to make sure he didn't do anything stupid.

"Remember, you say anything other than what I told you, I'll kill you right here."

Williams nervously nodded and finished dialing. After a couple rings, Steckenridge picked up. As Williams started talking, Jacobs took a few steps back and leaned his back against the wall. He made sure Williams could see he had his gun pointed at him in the event that he slipped up.

"Hey... Gnat," Williams said, trying to sound as upbeat as he could under the circumstances.

"What's up?"

"I just wanted to let you know I finished everything you guys needed."

"Already?"

"I've been working on it non-stop all day."

"OK? Is there a problem?" Steckenridge asked, not sure why he was calling. It was an accepted conclusion that everything would be done in a few days when they originally agreed to it. There was no need to call early unless there was an issue.

"Umm, well, just a small one."

"What is it?"

"Well, I have to go out-of-town tomorrow for an emergency," Williams said. "So, I'm afraid I need to get you this stuff tonight, in the next few hours if possible."

Steckenridge was a little put-off by the change in plans. He didn't like things not going according to schedule. It was a trait that he learned from his boss, Rich Mallette. They wanted things to go precisely according to plan. Any changes, even if it at first seemed positive, had the potential to screw things up.

"Why the rush?"

"Well, like I said, I have to leave town tomorrow so I won't be able to get these to you like we originally talked about," Williams said.

"The heat on you?"

"What? No, no. It's just a family thing. I have a, uh, cousin back in New York who's in some kind of trouble with the law. I have to try and figure things out."

"And you're sure everything's finished?" Steckenridge asked, still sounding unsure.

"Yeah, promise. Everything's good to go. I've been working overtime to make sure it's ready since I had to go away. If tonight's a problem, I can give them to an associate of mine to make the drop with you if you still wanted to keep it the same day."

Steckenridge thought about it for a few seconds, but that didn't sound that appealing to him either. He didn't want to meet anyone he didn't know or was familiar with. "No. I don't like new people. Especially in spots like this."

"I understand. Unless you want to postpone things until I get back."

"When will that be?"

"Tough to say. Probably five or six days at least. Maybe a week."

Steckenridge made a slight groan over the phone, barely loud enough to hear. Waiting a week or more wasn't a very alluring proposition either. "No. Tonight will be fine."

"Great. I'll bring everything and get you squared away. Do you want to name the place?"

As Williams finished his conversation, Jacobs put his gun away. Everything seemed to have gone smoothly. A few seconds later, Williams put the phone down on the table. Jacobs was eager to hear the rest of the details.

Williams could see that Jacobs was waiting for him to divulge the rest of the particulars and didn't need to be spurred on to spill anything else. He immediately spoke up. "Two hours."

"Where?"

"There's uh, an abandoned warehouse type place they have. I think it used to be some type of trucking business or something."

Jacobs' eyes lit up, knowing exactly where he was talking about. It was the very same building he'd already visited a few days prior to that. Once Williams gave him the address, it confirmed his suspicions. At the very least, Jacobs had an idea of the surroundings and didn't have to worry about what he was walking into. If he left within a few minutes, he could probably beat Mallette's gang over to it.

"Does Steckenridge or anybody else know you on sight?"

Williams shook his head, though he couldn't be sure of the answer. "I... I don't think so. I've never met any of them in person before. Whether they found a picture of me or something beforehand, I can't say."

"You know how many men are coming?" Jacobs asked.

"I'm not sure. It was never said."

"Well, how many people did you design stuff for?"

"Fifteen."

Jacobs was surprised at the number, not expecting it to be so large. Though he knew Mallette had more men than that, he figured only the top four or five would be leaving town. Having all the information he wanted, he had no further need of Williams.

"All right, you can go," Jacobs said.

Williams was a little surprised by it. He didn't get up at first and stayed planted in his seat, thinking he must've been playing with him or something. Jacobs didn't want to play games and waste time and spurred him on.

"C'mon, get your stuff and go."

"You really mean I can leave?" Williams asked.

"Before you go, I'm gonna give you some advice."

"OK?"

"You call them back and tell them about me, you're as good as dead," Jacobs said.

"I won't."

"Good. 'Cause I'll tell you, I have a friend who's gonna follow you. You're not gonna see him. And if he tells me something seems fishy, he'll kill you first. And if I get to that warehouse, and I think you set me up, I'll call him and have him kill you for me."

Williams took a big gulp, understanding what he was being warned of. "Believe me, I wanna get as far away from this as possible."

"I hope so. Because if I die, you're probably gonna die after me once they figure out you sold them out."

"I know that."

Jacobs nodded and gave Williams a pat on top of his shoulder. "Just wanted to make sure we understood each other and were on the same page."

"We are."

Williams grabbed his stuff and left the office and went to the back door, not even giving Franks a second look, or seeming to care about his situation. Once Jacobs locked the back door after Williams left, he came back to the office, finding Franks had already freed himself from the ropes.

With a smile on his face, Franks stood up, feeling proud he got out of his restraints without help. "Hey, look, getting pretty good at this."

"Wonderful."

"So, what's the plan, chief?"

"The plan is to go over there and kill as many of them as possible."

"You call that a plan?"

"Best I got," Jacobs answered. "Unless you wanna come over and help."

Franks put his hands up and took a few steps back. "Nuh uh, not me, man. This one's all on you. Remember, I'm a lover, not a fighter. Violence is your bag. You really gonna try and go up against fifteen of them?"

"I doubt there'll be that many. I figure there might be four or five, tops."

"And what if you're wrong?" Franks asked.

"Then I guess we'll have a heck of a battle, won't we?"

"I dunno, man, I'm not liking the odds for you."

"It'll be fine. If I leave now, I should be able to beat them there. I'll be able to see them come in. That'll give me the upper hand."

"Well, I wish you lots of luck, man. Hopefully, I won't be reading your obituary tomorrow."

16

WITH THE MEETING with Steckenridge set for 1 a.m., Jacobs left Franks' pawn shop only a few minutes after Williams did. With his bag full of weapons, Jacobs had enough firepower to chop down a platoon full of Mallette's men if it came down to that. Assuming they didn't overwhelm him with numbers before he was able to make that happen.

Jacobs got to the warehouse around midnight, the front gate still not locked from the last time he broke it. The chain was just wrapped around the gate to keep it closed. Jacobs made sure he parked several streets over so alarm bells wouldn't go off upon seeing a strange vehicle there. After going through the gate, Jacobs wrapped the chain around the poles again so Mallette's boys wouldn't be tipped off of his presence.

Without knowing exactly where Mallette's bunch was going to go, Jacobs had to set up in a position that would allow him to see the crew coming in, while also concealing his position, while also giving him defensive capabilities. He thought about the roof, but they could just surround it and make his escape almost impossible.

It was either wait in the office, or in the warehouse storage area. Jacobs wasn't sure they'd even go inside, but assumed they would, rather than doing business outside and in the view of any possible onlookers. If that was the case, it stood to reason they'd go into the office. Seeing as how he already broke open the door to the office the last time he was there, getting in again was a snap. Obviously, nobody had been there since then or it would have been fixed. Either that, or they just didn't care enough.

There was a separate entrance to the warehouse area, and Jacobs stood just behind the door, carefully watching the front gate. He had his bag on the floor, easily within reach should he need more firepower. Hopefully, he wouldn't need all of it, but he was already well prepared. He had two handguns in his belt, an assault rifle slung over his back, and another rifle in his hands. His hope was that he'd take the group by complete surprise and thoroughly inundate them with power and bullets before they even knew what hit them.

For close to an hour, Jacobs stood there, patiently waiting for his would-be victims to arrive. As he did, visions of Valerie flashed through his head. No matter what was about to happen, he knew his work wouldn't be finished there. It was unlikely all of Mallette's men would be there, and even if they were, Jacobs didn't think he could turn the switch off at that point. He couldn't go back to his former life. There was nothing to go back to. Family, job, friends, they were all gone now. He'd come to accept it. Even if this were the end of Mallette's bunch, he knew he'd have to move on to something else. Some other cause that drew his attention.

After a few minutes of allowing his mind to wander, Jacobs was able to refocus, knowing he had to have total concentration on the enemy force that he was about to face. Any lapse in that could mean his life. He wasn't going against a ragtag group of amateurs that barely knew how to handle a weapon. They were a seasoned group of hardened criminals, battle tested with years of experience under the tutelage of Rich Mallette. They wouldn't go down quietly.

Jacobs' concentration was broken again, this time by the sound of his phone ringing. It was about ten minutes to one. Since he wasn't expecting a call, he could only assume it was bad news. Maybe all his plans had gone up in smoke. Maybe his threats to Williams or Mills didn't work the way he was hoping or expecting them to. Maybe Steckenridge and his batch of friends knew he was there. A lot of maybes kept going through his mind, none of them very positive. As he looked at the phone before answering, he saw it was Franks. Jacobs assumed that he'd heard of a potential problem and was giving him a warning.

"Hey," Jacobs answered.

"How's everything going there?"

"Uh, fine. What's up?"

"Nothing, man, just wanted to make sure you were OK."

"Uh, yeah. Are you seriously telling me that's why you called?"

"Yeah, why?" Franks said.

"I'm sitting here waiting for a bunch of thugs to show up and you're calling me to shoot the breeze?"

"Wow, I'm sensing a lot of hostility here. Sue me for caring, man. I wasn't sure if the festivities started a little early or anything. Just wanted to make sure you weren't dead in a hail of bullets or anything."

"Well, even if I was, do you think I'd be answering right now?"

"All right, man, fair point, fair point. I can sense you're a little tense right now so I'll leave you to your own devices."

"Unbelievable," Jacobs said.

"Fine, if you're gonna act like that, I'm not gonna tell you the other thing."

"What other thing?"

"I'm sitting around the corner if you need a getaway car."

"You're what?"

"You got hearing problems?" Franks sarcastically asked. "I said..."

"I heard you. Why?"

"Why what?"

Jacobs felt like taking the phone and banging it against his head out of frustration. "Why are you sitting around the corner?"

"In case you got into a jam and you needed a quick exit."

"I'm not asking for your help in this and you don't have to get mixed up in it."

"Yeah, I know. I just figured I'd do a good deed."

Though Jacobs wasn't unhappy about having the help or Franks looking out for him, he didn't want him to get in over his head either. "This isn't your fight."

"I know, man, I know. Maybe you just strike a chord with me for some reason. I guess I'm just down with the cause."

"But it's my cause. Not yours."

"You sure have a strange way of saying thank you for the help," Franks said. "It's not like I have to be here or anything."

"Fine, but don't say I didn't warn you. If you die, it's your fault."

"Gee, thanks for sending the positive waves my way. You always so friendly with your comrades?"

"Just want you to know the stakes we're dealing with."

"Dude, I know who we're dealing with. Besides, I

figured by sitting out here I can give you a heads-up on when they're coming. They should be passing me soon."

"And you don't think they'll see you?" Jacobs asked.

"Nah, not me, man. This ain't my first time slinking down into the depths of a car passing by."

"Somehow that doesn't surprise me."

"Listen, soon as they roll in, I'm gonna head around to the back and wait out there for you."

"Why? What's back there?"

"There's a street in back, man. I thought you scouted this place out before?"

"Well, more or less just the inside," Jacobs answered. "Why don't you just stay out near the front gate?"

"'Cause if it gets hot and heavy and the police start rolling in, getting out of there's gonna be a bit of a challenge, don't you think?"

"And it won't be in back?"

"Nah, it's quiet back there."

"How do you know?"

"I've been here before... under various circumstances."

"So how do I get back there?" Jacobs asked.

"There's a small metal gate in the far left-hand corner of the property, really only big enough for a person to get through."

"As opposed to what?"

"Just listen. The gate's probably locked, so you either gotta bust through it or climb over it."

"How tall is it?"

"I think about eight feet," Franks replied.

There was silence on the phone between them for a minute before Franks hurriedly spoke out again.

"Oh, crap, they just passed me."

"Who?"

"I dunno, man, but it's two cars. Two big SUVs just rolled by. Should be at your location pronto."

Jacobs closed his eyes and shook his head, thinking that Franks sure knew how to dramatize a situation.

"You see how many were in there?"

"Nah, man, I was too busy ducking," Franks said. "You can bet they're probably jam-packed though."

"All right, thanks."

"See you around back, I hope."

Jacobs tightly gripped his weapon as he kept an eye out on the front gate. Within minutes, he saw a couple of cars pull up to it. A man got out of one of the cars and unwrapped the chains, pushing the gates open, not seeming concerned about the fact that it was broken. Once he was back in the car, they drove through the opening and pulled up to the front of the buildings. When the cars finally stopped, nobody got out of them for a few minutes. Jacobs wondered if they knew he was there, or maybe they were just being cautious. He hoped they wouldn't stay in there until they saw Williams appear or else it'd be a long wait. It

also would mean that he'd have a tougher time eliminating the group as he'd have to pepper the cars with
bullets.

With no movement around the cars for about five
minutes, all the doors to both cars suddenly and simul-
taneously started swinging open. Jacobs saw eight men
get out of the vehicles, four from each car. After closing
their respective doors, all the men milled around their
cars for a few minutes, looking around. Before he left
Franks' shop, they discussed whether Jacobs should
pretend to be Williams, that way he'd get up close to
them. Though the plan had some merit, if they already
knew what Williams looked like, they'd probably get to
shooting before Jacobs did. The bigger issue with that
was that Jacobs was only expecting four or five men.
Now that he saw there were eight, it was a slightly
bigger task than he had hoped for. Taking out four
men up close was doable, but eight would be a little
tougher equation.

After a few more minutes of standing around, the
men in the parking lot started stirring around. One of
the men got on a phone. Considering they weren't on it
long, maybe thirty seconds, Jacobs couldn't be sure if
they actually talked to someone, or maybe had just left
a message. He hoped they weren't calling Williams
before going in as that would throw off his plans.
Another minute went by and all the men came
together in a group, discussing something. If they
decided to get back in their cars and leave, then Jacobs

would have to come out blasting. He wasn't going to let them escape without a fight. Luckily, it didn't come to that. The men split up, with four of them staying outside, near the cars, while the other four went inside.

The men on the outside spread out a little bit, two staying near the cars, while the other two started walking around the perimeter of the grounds. Jacobs didn't know if they were specifically looking for trouble, or whether it was just a precautionary move. The other four went to the main office, and seeing the smashed door, got out their guns in case of trouble.

Jacobs figured it'd be easier to take out the men in the office first. He left his bag on the ground so he could come back to it later if he needed something in a hurry. He had enough firepower with what he had on him to get the first four. He slipped out of the side door of the warehouse that opened up to a long hallway that led to the office area. He quickly raced down the hallway, not wanting someone to spot him from the office before he was ready. Once he finally got to the door that led to the office, Jacobs stood to the side of it, listening at first.

"How long we gonna wait here?" one man asked.

"Till Williams gets here," Steckenridge firmly replied.

"What if that's not for an hour or so?"

"He said he'll be here. He'll be here."

"I don't like this. Something don't feel right," another man chimed in.

"What's the matter?" Steckenridge asked. "You afraid of the dark? Ghosts? Things that go bump in the night?"

"No. Just don't feel right. This guy tells us to meet him a day early, then when we get here, he ain't even here."

"He'll be here. Maybe he got lost in traffic."

"You don't think he's setting us up for something, do you?"

"Setting us up for what?"

"Cops?"

"You see any cops around?" Steckenridge asked.

"No."

"No, that's right. You know why? 'Cause he ain't stupid. He knows he'd be a dead man if he did that."

"I guess so."

"Jeez, you boys, lay low for a week and you start going stir crazy or something," Steckenridge said. "We picked the place, probably took a wrong turn in getting here. He'll probably be here in a few minutes. Relax."

Steckenridge put his gun away and sat down in the chair at the desk and put his feet up. He was calm as could be. There were no doubts in his mind that Williams would show up any minute. The rest of the men followed Steckenridge's actions and also put their guns away.

"So, what do you think happened to that door?" one of them asked.

"Yeah, that front gate was cut open too," another said.

Steckenridge waved them both off, not having a care in the world, or giving it a second thought. "Probably kids. You know how kids are. We haven't used this place in a couple of months."

"What would kids break in here for?"

"Why do kids do anything? For the thrill of it. Probably saw it was deserted and snuck in to see if they could steal anything. Or maybe they just came in for a place to smoke a joint in. Who knows?"

"You don't think someone's waiting for us or anything?"

Steckenridge laughed, thinking it was preposterous. "Man, you guys are really jumpy. It's a good thing the old man's locked up in prison right now or he'd be handing you your head for acting like this. If it makes you feel better, go search the place."

Jacobs took that as his cue. He didn't know whether they actually would search, but now was as good a time as any to unleash some payback. He made sure his rifle was ready to fire, and he quickly pushed open the door.

"Good idea. Maybe you should," Jacobs said, standing there in the door, big as life. Just like out of a movie.

Mallette's boys were stunned that the man was there. All of them recognized who he was. And they guessed why he was there. They started reaching for their guns, but Jacobs immediately opened fire, spreading the bullets around the room equally. He fired at a furious pace; the bodies dropping to the ground instantly. It only took a minute or two until it was over. Four dead bodies. Blood everywhere. It looked like a scene out of an old-time movie from 1930s Chicago.

Jacobs' blood was boiling, and he was on a high from the action. It seemed like he was a transformed man. The mild-mannered, easy-going guy he usually was, was now possessed by some gun-toting, enraged, drugged up maniac. It was almost like an out-of-body experience. It probably had to do with finally getting a chance to extract some revenge on his family's murderers. Here he was, looking right at them, and sending them down into their own path of hell.

Remembering that there were more outside, Jacobs went over to the smashed-up door and peeked outside. Two of the men started running toward the office, guns in hand, to see what was going on. Jacobs made himself visible in the doorway and started blasting away. The man in front went down right away. The man behind him was able to get off a few shots, though none hit Jacobs. Without having any protection between him and the gun-happy man at the door, the man didn't have much of a chance. Jacobs easily mowed him down. That left two more.

Jacobs was still on a high. In his amped up state, he probably could have continued doing this for another hour or two. He didn't want to stop. He wanted Mallette's men to keep coming. He wished more would have come crashing through the gate so he wouldn't have to stop. He could keep on fighting. He wouldn't have to postpone anything for a future time. He could get it all over with in one night. But he knew that wouldn't happen. But he was making the best of the circumstances as he could.

Jacobs peeked his head out the door, trying to find the last two members of the group. He couldn't see where they were. Maybe they took off. Or maybe they were hiding somewhere. Or maybe they were entering the building from another spot. The more he thought about it, he figured it was likely they were somewhere else. With the amount of bodies that were now in the office area, and just outside it, they probably wouldn't try to enter right there, knowing how the others wound up.

From being there before, Jacobs remembered there was a back door in the rear of the warehouse. He quickly retreated from the office and ran down the hallway until he entered the warehouse again. He took a quick look around to see if he had company before he fully entered the space. Seeing that he was alone so far, he scurried to the back of the warehouse until he came to another door. This one led to another hallway that housed a few more rooms. They were used for offices, break rooms, janitorial supplies, and other miscellaneous purposes.

Instead of waiting there in the hallway in plain sight, Jacobs looked to one of the other rooms and slipped inside. He flipped on the light switch and saw it was the break room. There was a long table, some chairs, and a few vending machines. Seeing how much dirt and dust was there, it must not have been used much even when the place was occupied. He then turned the lights off. Jacobs wasn't sure how long he'd wait there, but probably not too long, since he wasn't sure they were even coming in that way. Maybe they would come through the front after all. Or maybe with all the commotion, they just figured it was a lost cause and left. But considering the cars were still there, he dismissed that as unlikely. They probably wouldn't escape on foot. He stood next to the door, leaving it open just a hair so he could peek through the crack and see someone walking past.

His questions were soon answered as he heard the back door jiggle open. A few cracks were heard in the floorboards. Several were heard, a few seconds apart, indicating to Jacobs that both men were coming in. There were a couple of doors on both sides of the hallway before the men got to the break room. Jacobs observed the one man sneak into one of the rooms, presumably to make sure he wasn't in one of them. That meant they'd be checking the one he was in soon. He gently put down his assault rifle on the floor, being careful that it didn't make a sound once it hit the concrete. He then removed his Glock pistol from his belt and made sure it was ready for action.

As he waited for his visitors, Jacobs knelt on his right knee and aimed his pistol up. He held that position for a minute until the door swung open. As soon as the man entering the room put his hand on the light switch and flicked it on, Jacobs opened fire. The man barely saw Jacobs at the last second, but it was far too late to react. The bullet pierced through the man's neck and ended up in his skull. The blood from his neck wound splattered against the wall, the man dying as he hit the ground.

Knowing the second man would be on him in a second, Jacobs sprung out the door. The other man rushed out of the room he was checking just a few seconds after Jacobs got into the hallway. Jacobs readied his arms in front of him, and as soon as he saw the outline of the second man, blasted him with three rounds in the chest, knocking him onto his back as his shirt quickly became stained red. Seeing the last remaining member of the group on the ground and eliminated, Jacobs finally allowed himself to breathe. He wiped the sweat from his face, and he slowly started to calm down. The high he was on was evaporating, knowing there was no one else to kill. At least for the moment.

Jacobs stood in the hallway, looking at the two dead bodies, almost not knowing what to do next. He remembered what Franks told him about meeting him in the back and figured he should split the scene. He walked back into the warehouse area and found his bag. He put his guns back into it and slung it over his shoulder as he readied to leave. Even though a small piece inside of him was happy with how the events transpired, he still had a sullen look on his face. He was satisfied with this battle, but the war wasn't over yet. There were still other players at large. Especially Frazier. The man who pulled the trigger.

As Jacobs thought about what just transpired, he knew it was likely one of two things would happen. The rest of Mallette's gang would get shaken up by the killings and bury themselves even deeper into whatever hole they were hiding in, making it tougher and longer for Jacobs to find them. Or, they could get angry about it, and come out of hiding, looking for the man responsible and want to make an example out of him. He actually hoped it was the latter. And nothing would make him happier.

He was about to head into the hallway that led to the rear of the building, but stopped when an idea flashed into his head. Jacobs thought maybe one of them was carrying something that would lead him to the rest of their group. Then he thought of their cell phones. If he checked each of their call logs, maybe he could trace the numbers of their friends back to their location. It was at least worth a shot. He eagerly went back to the main office. Now that the rush had worn off, he felt bad for a few seconds that he was the one who did it. But fleeting thoughts of Val and the kids rushed across his mind, quickly ending any sorrowful thoughts he had about committing the heinous acts.

Jacobs quickly checked the dead men's pockets one by one and removed each of their cell phones, stuffing them in his weapons bag. He started checking their pockets for anything else that he might find useful, maybe a piece of paper with a name or an address. Those pursuits were quickly cut short though. His eyes glanced through the opened door that led outside and saw the flashing lights of police cars. They were just pulling through the main gate. Two of them. Someone must have heard the shots and called.

Jacobs knew he didn't have any more time to check the victims for anything else. At least he had their phones though. That was something. He raced back through the hallway and the warehouse, hoping there wouldn't be another patrol car parked in the back of the building. As he ran through the hall that led to the back door, Jacobs stopped, taking a few seconds to remove the phones of the last two dead men. After quickly throwing them in his bag, he went out the back door.

He stood there for a few seconds, making sure he wasn't running straight into the police. With the coast seeming clear, Jacobs broke for the back fence, running for the corner gate as Franks suggested. Once he got there, the gate was padlocked. Jacobs anxiously looked back, hoping nobody was on his tail. Everything still seemed quiet, almost like nothing had just happened inside. He knew he didn't have time to play around with the lock and threw his bag over the fence. Then, he took a few steps back and took a running leap for the middle of the fence. Grabbing a firm hold of it, he climbed up the rest of it, falling back down on the other side.

Before leaving, Jacobs took one last look at the warehouse. Still, nobody was coming. He then started running for the street, passing through some back-yards and houses until he came to the street. Once he got there, he saw a blue car running with its lights on. It had to be Franks. He quickly ran over to it and looked in the window, seeing it was him in the driver's seat. Jacobs opened the door and threw his bag on the floor. As soon as he was in, Franks floored it, racing out of the area.

"Whooo, looks like you got out just in time, my friend," Franks happily exclaimed. "They are converging on that place like I don't know what."

Jacobs looked down and saw a radio tuned in to listen to the police band. "Always carry that with you?"

"Comes in handy, man. Comes in handy."

"I bet."

"So, how'd it go?"

"I'm here."

"Yeah, but how many of them did you get?" Franks asked.

"Eight."

"Eight?! Wow, that's some good shooting right there."

Not really impressed with the number, Jacobs had other things on his mind. "You sure this thing is safe?"

Franks looked at him strangely. "What're you talking about? This is a sound car."

"I don't mean that. You sure nobody's gonna call it in if they saw it leave back there?"

"Oh, that. No need to worry about that, my friend."

"Why not?"

"Even if someone calls in the license plate, it won't come back to this car anyway."

"Oh. What if they just give out a description?"

"Also no need to fret. We'll be ducking into a little auto garage place I know of," Franks replied. "Owner's a friend of mine."

"You do know someone just about everywhere, don't you?"

"It pays to have friends in the right places, man."

Jacobs leaned back in his seat and closed his eyes. He was reflecting on what he'd just done. Eight bodies. And that was on top of the ones he killed in the days before. It almost didn't seem real. He was doing it so easily, without thought. Suddenly, doubts about what he was doing crept into his mind. Was he becoming a monster? Just a killer? Was this the beginning of turning into a man he wouldn't even recognize? And if he was, was it worth it? Was it worth it to extract justice and revenge for the death of his family? He heard

Franks saying something, but he was zoning out and not focusing on him, so he really didn't hear what he was saying. Eventually, Franks' voice broke through.

"Hey, man, you listening?"

"What?"

"I said, anything else happen? Other than the shootings, I mean? Find out anything?"

"Uh, no, no words were spoken," Jacobs said.

"That's too bad."

Jacobs reached down and pulled his bag up onto his lap. He opened it up and pulled out a couple cell phones. "I did take these off of each of them, though. I'm hoping something on here turns up."

A confident look sprung up on Franks' face. "You know what? If there's something on there to be found, we'll find it. I got a guy."

A devilish smile overtook Jacobs' face. "I was hoping you'd say that."

17

TWO DAYS HAD PASSED since the incident at the Mallette warehouse. Jacobs had given all the cell phones he took to Franks to have his friend look at them. He could have tried doing it himself by trying to trace the call log numbers, but he figured Franks' contact would probably do it better and quicker. While he waited for a call to let him know everything was done, Jacobs went back to his old house to look for the packages that he'd ordered. When he pulled up, it felt a little weird being there again. Even though he'd only been gone a few days, it looked different somehow. Almost like it was someone else's house.

After sitting in his car for a few minutes staring at the house, Jacobs finally got out of the car. He saw the packages near the front and walked up the steps. As he picked the boxes up and turned around, he saw a car pull up. He continued walking down the steps as

Buchanan got out and started coming towards him. Once Jacobs got near the bottom of the steps, he just put the boxes down and sat next to them. Considering there were no patrol cars with Buchanan, he assumed he wasn't being arrested yet. He stared straight ahead as he waited for the sergeant to explain why he was there. Buchanan walked up a couple of steps, then sat next to his friend.

"Where you been?" Buchanan asked.

"Out."

"Oh. Was here earlier and saw you weren't home. Yesterday too."

"Been busy."

"Where's your car?"

Jacobs wanted to kick himself for already getting his new car made. "Oh, it's, uh, in the shop. Getting an oil change."

"Oh. So, where you going with those boxes?"

"I was just about to walk down to get the car."

"What's in them?" Buchanan asked.

"Just ordered a new coat."

"Nice."

"So, what are you here for?" Jacobs asked. "I'm sure you're not here to talk about my car or my new coat or the weather or any of that other nonsense."

"Just wanted to see how you were doing, how you're holding up."

"I'm good."

"You make it sound that easy."

"Well, gotta move on, right?"

"We miss you downtown."

Jacobs threw his arms up. "It is what it is now."

"So, you heard about any of the stuff been going down the last couple days?"

Buchanan carefully studied his friend's face as he answered. Jacobs, though, didn't give off any clues that he knew what he was talking about. He shook his head. "No. What's been happening?"

"Looks like someone took out some of Mallette's boys the other day."

"No kidding?"

"Yeah, eight of them went down in one of Mallette's old warehouses."

"Well, can't say I'm sorry it happened or that I feel bad for them or anything," Jacobs said.

"You don't happen to know anything about it, do you?"

"Me? No. First I've heard of it, actually. Didn't catch the people who did it?"

"No, not yet. We're still sifting through things, working leads, you know."

"Any cameras, witnesses, or anything?"

Buchanan shook his head and sounded frustrated, though he really wasn't. "No. There were reports of shots being fired, but by the time patrol cars got there, all they found were dead bodies."

"Well, maybe something will turn up."

"Usually does. Just hope it doesn't turn up anything... that might be troubling."

"Such as?" Jacobs asked, getting the hint that he was being referred to.

"I think you know."

"I don't know what you're talking about."

The two sat there silently for a minute, looking out into the distance and watching a few cars pass by. Then Jacobs spoke up, thinking of a plan that might get Buchanan looking in a new direction.

"Hey, remember that other thing you told me about? The shootings at the, uh... what was it? Dry cleaner or something?"

"Yeah."

"Maybe this is connected to that."

"You think so?"

"Could be. Wasn't there another shooting or something? Down the street from the dry cleaner. A, uh, pawn shop or something?"

Buchanan nodded, seeing where he was going with it. "Yeah, yeah. The same gang that used the dry cleaner store as a front as a matter of fact."

Jacobs tilted his head and raised his hand slightly. "Maybe that's it. They got hit twice. Maybe Mallette's group was the one responsible for both hits. The warehouse job was payback."

"Yeah, yeah, I guess that's one possibility. A couple of the boys downtown actually floated that same theory around."

"There you go."

"Well, we still haven't found any connection between the two groups."

"Doesn't mean there isn't one."

"True, true. Of course, the one gang's leader, Ronnie Cedeno, he was killed in the pawn shop job."

"There you go. Good motive. Mallette's bunch killed their leader, they hit them back for revenge," Jacobs said.

"I suppose it could've happened like that."

After a few more minutes of silence, Buchanan knew he wasn't going to get anything else out of his friend. Though he couldn't prove that Jacobs had a hand in any of the stuff that'd been going down, he had that nagging feeling that he was knee-deep into it. He just couldn't shrug off that some of Mallette's bunch had been killed just a week after Jacobs quit the force. It seemed like an awfully big coincidence to him. But, he needed evidence, and he didn't have it. Not one shred.

"Well, I guess I'll be moving on," Buchanan said, tapping Jacobs on the knee as he got up.

"Good luck with your cases."

"Thanks. You keep on staying out of trouble, huh?"

"You know it."

Buchanan got back in his car and drove away. Once Jacobs saw he was out of the picture, he got up and put his boxes in his new car. He didn't bother opening them until he got to his new place. He was just about ready to try them on when his phone rang. It was Franks.

"Hey."

"Hey, what's happening cutie?" Franks said with a laugh. Jacobs didn't respond. "I was, uh, just joking there."

Jacobs found him slightly amusing but thought it was better not to show it so as not to encourage him with his silly jokes. "I know."

"Yeah, well, anyway, boy do we got some news for you."

"OK?"

"Well, come down to the shop and I'll tell you all about it. You know I don't like to discuss business over the telephono."

"All right. I'll be right down."

When Jacobs got to the pawn shop, he entered through the back, like he was starting to become accustomed to. Franks immediately led him to the office.

"You got any customers out front?" Jacobs asked.

"Nah, I put the closed for lunch sign up on the door," Franks replied, waving him off like he didn't even worry about it.

As they walked into the office, Jacobs saw a new person sitting at the desk, working on a laptop.

Franks immediately introduced them. "Brett, this is Hack. Hack, Brett."

"Hack?" Jacobs asked.

"Yeah, well, it's more of a nickname, but you don't really need to know his real name," Franks replied. "Everyone just calls him Hack."

"Why?"

"'Cause he's good at hacking. Why else?"

"Oh. So, what's he hacking into?"

"Your future," Hack replied.

"What?"

"I've gone so next level."

Jacobs' eyes darted around the room, before turning his head to look at Franks, wondering what the hell the kid was talking about. Hack looked like he was barely twenty years old and that might have been pushing it. Franks could tell that Jacobs already had reservations but put his hand up to let him know everything was cool.

"You wanna tell me what's going on?" Jacobs asked.

"Oh, OK," Franks said. "So, I gave the phones to Hack to analyze, which he did."

"Nothing to it really," Hack replied.

"Yeah. So, he hacked some stuff, and got into some stuff, which led to some other stuff, which then went into some other stuff."

Jacobs forcefully put his hand on Franks' arm to get him to stop talking nonsense. "What are you saying?"

"Oh, well, basically, we found out where Frazier is," Franks said nonchalantly.

Jacobs almost couldn't believe it. "What?"

"Yeah, we pinned him down."

Jacobs took a look at Hack, who peeked up at him from behind his laptop and nodded, affirming it.

"How?" Jacobs asked.

Hack spoke up to explain the entire process. "Well, it all emanated from the phone contacts lists. See, they all had basically the same numbers in there, which I was able to trace to a certain location."

"OK?"

"Well, that was pretty easy, child's play, actually. I mean, anybody could've done that. I had that done like a few hours after I got the phones. Nothing to it."

"And the location?"

"Well, looking through the phones, some of them had sent emails, I mean, none of them had any sort of protection or encryption or anything, it was almost like these guys were just begging to be hacked, I mean, really."

"The location?" Jacobs repeated.

"Well, anyway, I traced the phone numbers and the emails, and yada, yada, yada, it all came back to one place."

"Which is?"

"A bar on the south side," Hack answered.

"OK. So how does that place Frazier there?"

Instead of explaining it, Hack just spun his computer around so that Jacobs could take a look, figuring he'd get a better understanding of it that way. As Jacobs looked at the information, he could visualize what Hack was saying. The numbers, the emails, they were all tracing back to one location and one name. It was a name that Hack had figured out was just a fake name that Frazier concocted to try and conceal himself.

"You know that place?" Franks asked.

"Actually, I do," Jacobs replied. "There was talk a while ago that Mallette owned it, but it wasn't something that could be proven. Nothing was in his name. He'd gone there a lot, but like I said, couldn't prove that he actually owned it."

"Well, I hacked into the records of the building and plans and all that," Hack said. "And it looks like there's a second floor to the bar."

"Upstairs apartments?"

"Yeah. Looks like a couple of them, actually. There's staircases leading down to the back alley."

"One's probably the bar owner," Franks said.

"Yeah, I'd say the other one is probably rented out. Either that or it's a meeting place for Mallette, or maybe a spare room to hide people out in when the heat's on, stuff like that."

Jacobs nodded. It all sounded good. It all made sense.

"What are you gonna do?" Franks asked.

Jacobs looked at Hack, not wanting to reveal anything in front of him. Franks could see that he was nervous about talking with Hack around and sought to ease his mind.

"It's OK, you can talk in front of him. He knows all about it."

Jacobs tilted his head and raised his eyebrows, giving Franks a look of disapproval.

"Do you always tell everyone else my business?" Jacobs asked.

"What? What's the big deal?"

"Because the less people who know about me and my plans, the less chance there is of me being known or caught."

"What? Hack? You don't have to worry about him," Franks said. "Besides, if he wanted to, he could find everything out on his own in like thirty seconds anyway."

"He's right, man," Hack said. "You ain't gotta worry about me, I'm down with the cause."

"You are?"

"Yeah, Hack isn't in this for money or anything like the rest of us," Franks said.

"Is that right?"

"Nah, I'm all about hacking for good," Hack said. "I don't do it for evil purposes."

"Is that so?"

"Yeah. I'm all about hacking for justice, for social issues, making the world a better place, doing the right thing, things like that. Man, ridding the world of creeps like Mallette's gang is justice as far as I'm concerned."

"So glad you approve," Jacobs said.

"Yeah, some of the stuff I've uncovered about that group. You just wouldn't believe it."

Jacobs gave him a glare, not believing he just said that. Realizing what he said was stupid, Hack looked back up at him. "Well, I guess maybe you would."

"So, what's the plan this time?" Franks asked.

"I don't think I really need to say, do I?"

"Well, before you go charging in there, you better make sure he's there, don't you think?"

"Nah, I can do you better," Hack said.

"How's that?" Jacobs replied.

"You just leave it to me."

As Hack was doing his thing, whatever that entailed, Jacobs went back outside to his car and removed his bag, as well as the two packages he received. Once he came back into the office, he put the boxes on the ground and opened them. Franks was intrigued by the items and knelt next to Jacobs as he inspected them.

"Wow. Nice!" Franks exclaimed, feeling the vest.

Jacobs tried the coat on first. As he did, Franks came over to it and started tapping on it, trying to feel the armored plates.

"I like it," Franks said.

Jacobs then took it off and put it down. Then he put on the vest. Franks took a step back, analyzing him.

"Looks good, man."

"Feels pretty good," Jacobs said. "Some vests are

rather uncomfortable to wear, but this one is surprisingly all right."

Franks put his hand in a few of the pockets. "Looks like you got room for a bunch of cool gadgets and toys."

Hack glanced away from his work, taking a brief look at Jacobs. "Looks like you're about to go to war in that."

"I am."

18

IT WAS JUST past ten o'clock and Jacobs, Franks, and Hack were in the office of the pawn shop, going over some last-minute details. Jacobs had put his vest on again, ready to finish the fight. Though there were still more of Mallette's crew roaming around, this was the one who really mattered to him. Frazier was the one who pulled the trigger. He was the one who Jacobs had been aiming for. Everyone else was just a stepping stone to get to this point.

Jacobs felt calm, but anxious at the same time. He sat in a chair and looked straight ahead, looking at nothing but the wall. He tried to envision what his encounter with Frazier would be like. He went over it in his mind over and over again. After a few minutes, his concentration was broken by Franks.

"It's almost time, man."

Jacobs only nodded.

"Just out of curiosity, why you doing this, anyway?" Franks asked.

"Doing what?"

"This whole thing."

"Thought I explained all that already."

"Well, you told me the basic reason, but there must be something else behind that. I mean, why throw away your career for it? Why not let the law do its thing?"

"Because the law won't work for this," Jacobs answered.

"Why not? Thought Frazier was on video? Isn't that pretty spot-on evidence right there?"

"Yeah, but that doesn't get the man who ordered him to do it, or anyone else who helped him along with it, and Frazier would never talk. Plus, it's an organization thing. I think I told you this before. I don't want to see them behind bars. Jail's too good for them. I want to see them in the ground."

Their talk was then interrupted by Hack. "All right, it's done."

Jacobs got up, ready to move. "You're sure this will work?"

"Absolutely."

"Uh, just so I know for my own purposes what's going on, you mind repeating, like, how this is going down?" Franks asked.

Hack took a deep breath before responding. "OK. I analyzed all the information and phone numbers and all that and found one was coming from the prison that Rich Mallette was sent to, right?"

"Right."

"So that means he's got a way of communicating to his men from the inside, right? You follow me so far?"

"I'm right there with you, hoss."

"So, I devised a hack, or a spoof, that sent Frazier a message, disguising it to make it look like it came from Mallette."

"And he bought it?" Franks asked.

Hack quickly nodded several times, surprised he even asked the question. "Yeah, he did. No reason not to. It's a sound plan."

"Still seems kind of risky to me."

"Look, thanks to maps, we've seen the layout of that building. It's what, twenty, thirty steps until you reach that second-floor apartment? You'll never get there on your own."

"He's right," Jacobs said. "They'll start shooting anybody they don't recognize going up those steps."

"I dunno, man, just telling them in advance a police officer's coming seems kind of iffy," Franks said.

"It's the only way they'll let a stranger get closer. There's no doubt Mallette's already heard about what happened at the warehouse, right?" Hack asked.

"Right."

"So, I disguised a message pretending to be from him, telling Frazier that Mallette has a police contact on the inside who's on the payroll, who'll help them slip out of the city. It's perfect. It'll work. The only way you'll get someone close to him is if it's ordered from the boss and makes them think they're getting help."

"And what if they recognize who he is as he's walking up?" Franks replied. "I mean, it's not like he's a stranger to them."

"It's a chance I'll take," Jacobs said.

Hoping to help the odds a little bit, Franks walked over to a shelf and moved a few small boxes out of the way. He then grabbed a blue baseball hat and handed it to Jacobs. "Here, hope that helps."

Jacobs looked at it for a second, not sure about putting it on.

"Please, just humor me, would you?" Franks said.

"Well, it's about that time," Jacobs said.

"You come back in one piece, all right? Listen to me, I sound like an old worrywart mother or something."

Jacobs started to leave the office, but turned around as he hit the door. He knew this moment wouldn't have been possible unless he had help. And he'd gotten a lot of it up to that point. Much more than he ever could have hoped for. And he was grateful for it.

"Hey, uh, I... I just wanted to say thank you. To both of you. This means a lot to me and I appreciate all the help."

"You can thank me by paying me," Franks said.

"You can thank me by coming back in one piece," Hack said.

"Yeah, ditto that. 'Cause I ain't coming to your funeral, man."

Jacobs smiled, hoping Franks wouldn't have to. Jacobs then left through the back door and hopped in his car. He drove straight to the bar. He looked at the time and continued sitting in his car for a while, having about twenty minutes to go until the meeting. He had to give it to Hack. Jacobs thought it was a really clever plan he concocted. Telling Frazier that a cop on the take would come up to his apartment and help relocate him, after what happened to Steckenridge, was a bold plan, but one he thought would work. The only issue Jacobs could see was if Frazier knew it didn't come from his boss. But he figured if that was the case, then Frazier would probably not even be there now. If he thought it was the cops setting him up, he probably wouldn't stick around and wait. He'd most likely already have high-tailed it somewhere else.

Really, the only other issue that Jacobs could see was that he didn't know exactly how many men were with Frazier. In the message that Hack sent, he told him to bring two or three guys with him. Hopefully, he listened. They figured if they told him to bring a couple people with him, it would give him less reason to question and worry about anything. They thought if they said to make sure he was alone, that would give him some reason to panic or worry that he was being set-up.

The time went by quickly and twenty minutes

came in what seemed like a blink of an eye. As he got out of the car, he adjusted his vest, making sure it was positioned properly. He then put his coat on top of the vest. If he got into a gun battle, at least his major parts were protected. Unless they shot him in the head. Jacobs walked around the bar until he got to the back. He immediately saw the wooden steps that led up to the second-floor unit. As he walked closer to the steps, he noticed a light was on inside the apartment.

Jacobs stood at the base of the steps and looked at the apartment one more time. He lowered his hat down to try and conceal his face more. He adjusted his vest one more time, and he felt to make sure he had his guns in the right position. Knowing it'd be tough to conceal a rifle, and thinking they'd get alarmed if they saw him come up with one, he only brought handguns with him. Four of them. He started ascending the steps, a little nervous, hoping he didn't get shot on the way up. He was also a little anxious, hoping to finally kill the man who murdered his family.

By the time he got to the top of the steps, he heard some movement inside the apartment. It was likely they were watching him the whole time. He put his hand up to knock, but it wasn't necessary. Before his hand hit the door, it started to open. Only a crack. Half a man's face appeared through the slit, sizing Jacobs up and down.

"You the cop?"

"That's right," Jacobs said.

After a few seconds of staring at him, the man finally opened the door further. "Come on in."

Jacobs came in and quickly looked the room over to see how many men were in it. Besides the man at the door, there was another one sitting on the couch to his left. No sign of Frazier, though. The man at the door closed it, then lit a cigarette as he walked to the middle of the room.

"So exactly how are you going to help us?"

Jacobs continued looking around. "This all of you? Just you two?"

"No, Lucky's freshening up. He'll be out in a minute."

Jacobs nodded, then started walking around the room.

"So, what are you gonna do?" the man asked again.

"I'd rather wait till the other guy comes out so I can tell you all at the same time. I hate repeating myself."

The man took a drag of his cigarette and shrugged. Neither of them seemed all that concerned with Jacobs, and he was a little surprised they weren't watching him more closely. They didn't frisk him either. He supposed it was the power of Mallette recommending him, that they thought it was all on the up-and-up.

"Hey Lucky, c'mon. Let's get this thing over with."

"I'll be out in a minute," Frazier shouted back. "Keep your pants on."

The man with the cigarette seemed annoyed that

they had to wait as he stood in the middle of the room. Jacobs contemplated whether he should start shooting now or wait until Frazier came into the room. If he waited, he'd have three men to deal with. If he started now, he could easily pick off the two in front of him, neither of whom seemed threatened by him. But then he might wind up in a stand-off with Frazier. But he also knew that Frazier had nowhere to go. There was nowhere for him to run. In the end, Jacobs felt like it was better to deal with one man than three.

"Well, we might as well get this thing started," Jacobs said.

He removed one of the guns from his coat and fired two times at the man with the cigarette, hitting him point blank in the chest. As he was falling over, Jacobs took aim at the man on the couch, who was reading a magazine. The man wasn't able to react quick enough and withdraw his own gun before Jacobs blew several holes in him, one of which went through the magazine before ending up in the man's body. As he slumped over on the couch, Jacobs turned his attention to the hallway.

Just as he did, he saw Frazier come flying into the room. Jacobs got off a few rounds. As Frazier came crashing down onto the floor, he fired a couple of shots at Jacobs, one of which hit him in the thigh. Jacobs flinched slightly at the pinching pain that was coming from his leg, but shrugged it off and returned fire as Frazier tried to take cover behind a chair. Jacobs fired a few more rounds into the fabric of the chair, hoping it would find its mark.

Not sure how much ammunition he had left in his gun, Jacobs quickly took out his backup weapon and commenced firing. He hurried over to the side of the room, trying to get a better angle on his target. As he was doing it, Frazier sprung up from behind the chair, making a break for the front door. As he was running, he fired off a few rounds in Jacobs' direction. Jacobs dropped to a knee and returned fire, hitting Frazier several times, knocking him to the ground.

Seeing that Frazier wasn't dead yet, his arms were still moving, reaching for his gun which dropped out of his hand a few inches away from him, Jacobs rushed over to him. He kicked the gun further away from Frazier's hand and stood over him. Frazier puffed, knowing he'd lost the battle. He rolled over onto his back and looked up at his assailant. He didn't get a great look at him before, but now that he saw Jacobs up close, he let out a small laugh.

"It's you."

"It's me," Jacobs replied.

"Looks like we underestimated you."

"Looks like."

"Nothing personal, man. It was just business."

"Not for me," Jacobs said, pointing his gun at him.

Knowing he was done for, Frazier hoped for a quick death. "Just do it."

Something was pulling at Jacobs not to do it. At

least not yet. Frazier didn't deserve to be put out of his misery so quickly. Judging by the blood that was coming out of his body, it looked like he'd been hit in the leg and the shoulder. Neither of which was life-threatening, at least not yet. Not until he suffered a significantly larger amount of blood loss. But Jacobs was determined to make sure that happened. Frazier wasn't going to skate out of there under any circumstances.

"You the one who took out Gnat and them the other day?"

Jacobs nodded. "Yep."

Frazier laughed again. "Should've known." After another minute, Frazier was starting to get impatient at his ultimate fate. "What are you waiting for? You know you want to. Just do it."

"I do want to. Very badly. But I also want you to suffer. You killed my wife and children. I want you to be in an unbearable amount of pain. Something you're obviously not in yet."

Frazier, laughing again, didn't think Jacobs could pull off the torture routine. Frazier didn't think he had it in him. Tired of seeing the man laugh, Jacobs fired his weapon, putting another bullet in Frazier's leg, this time shattering his shin. Frazier screamed out in agony, clutching at his leg.

"What's the matter?" Jacobs asked. "Not so funny anymore?"

Frazier glared up at him, huffing and puffing, trying

to control his breathing from the agony he was in. As he was doing that, Jacobs shot him in the right shoulder, making it a matching set with the bullet in the other one.

"You fu..."

Jacobs wasn't in the mood to hear any more of his lip and fired another round, this time into the thigh of his leg. As Frazier screamed, and uttered curse words, he rolled around in pain.

"Feel the pain yet?" Jacobs asked. "No? How 'bout one more?"

Jacobs fired another round, this time the bullet lodging into Frazier's foot.

"Looks like you're losing an awful lot of blood," Jacobs said. "Somebody should probably get you to a hospital."

Frazier was able to block out the pain just long enough to utter a few more words. "No matter what you do, you can't bring them back. You can kill me fifty times here, you can't bring them back."

"I know it," Jacobs said, gritting his teeth.

Jacobs took aim one more time. This time, he fired directly at Frazier's testicles, hoping it'd cause him the most pain he'd ever felt in his life. His goal was accomplished, as Frazier let out the most horrifying scream that Jacobs had ever heard before. It would have been the perfect sound effect for a horror movie. After another minute of listening to Frazier holler, Jacobs thought his time was done there. He'd done what he sought to do. Now it was time to finish it. He raised his gun up, putting it only a few inches away from Frazier's forehead. He waited for Frazier to look at him. Jacobs wanted him to see it coming. Once Frazier did, Jacobs pulled the trigger, ending the life of his family's murderer. Blood splattered up and hit Jacobs in the face, but he hardly noticed. All he could see at that moment was that his work was finished.

After staring at the dead body for a minute, Jacobs stumbled back a few steps, almost unsure what to do next. With all the excitement, it felt like he had more work to do. But it was all done. Now, his thoughts turned to exiting. Surely other people heard the shots by now. The police were most likely on their way, he thought. He quickly exited, standing just outside the door at the top of the steps. An ever-growing crowd was starting to develop on the streets. Not wanting to be recognized, Jacobs knew he had to get past them somehow. And he had to do it quickly before the cops arrived.

Not knowing another way, Jacobs fired a few more rounds into the air, aiming toward the ground away from all the spectators. His only goal was to scare everyone away. This way he knew he wouldn't hit anybody, even by accident. Once the shots were fired, everyone down below started screaming and running for cover. As they did, Jacobs hustled down the steps. Once he was on the ground, he put his gun away and walked around to the front parking lot. As a couple of police cars rolled past, Jacobs hopped in his car and quickly peeled out of the lot.

Jacobs drove around for close to an hour, not really having any clear destination in mind. He didn't want to go back to his new place just yet. Not while all the festivities were fresh in his mind. He wanted everything to sink in a little first. It didn't seem real yet. Though he felt a small sense of satisfaction for eliminating the people that he did, it didn't bring back his family.

Eventually, Jacobs wound up at a familiar place. He stopped as he noticed he was in the back alley of Eddie's Pawn Shop. Maybe it was by accident, or maybe he'd been there so frequently lately that it just seemed like the right place to go. He wasn't even sure that Franks was still there. But he got out of the car and buzzed in anyway. After a minute, the door opened. Franks stood there, a big smile on his face, though he was a little concerned about Jacobs' appearance.

"You look like a mess, dude."

"You should see the other guy," Jacobs quipped.

"Yeah, I bet. You got blood on your face and everything, man."

Jacobs wiped his face with the sleeve of his coat. "Better?"

"Slightly. Come on in and get cleaned off."

Jacobs limped in and Franks observed the hole in his leg, with the blood that came along with it. After closing the door, Franks started questioning him on what happened. After Jacobs was through explaining everything, he sat down, finally feeling a small sense of peace.

"Probably need someone to take care of this," Jacobs said, pointing to his leg.

A wide smile came over Franks' face. "Don't worry. I got a guy."

Jacobs grinned. "I knew you would."

ABOUT THE AUTHOR

Mike Ryan is the popular crime fiction author of several bestselling books, including The Silencer Series, The Eliminator Series, The Cain Series, as well as several standalone titles. Visit his website, sign up for his newsletter, and find out more about his books at www.mikeryanbooks.com.

facebook.com/MikeRyanAuthor
instagram.com/mikeryanauthor

ALSO BY MIKE RYAN

Start reading book 2 of The Eliminator Series here:

The Payback

Start reading The Silencer Series here:

The Silencer

Start reading The Extractor Series here:

The Extractor

Other books by Mike Ryan:

The Brandon Hall Series

The Cain Series

The Ghost Series

A Dangerous Man

The Last Job

The Crew

Printed in Great Britain
by Amazon